MW01537987

Stories

from the

Early Morning

Thomas Zachek

Ellen ~
To my music -
making friend
Hope you enjoy!
Tom Zachil

© 2015 by Thomas Zachek. All rights reserved. No part of this book may be used or reproduced in any form without the express permission of the author or his heirs, except in the case of brief quotations embodied in critical articles and reviews. For information, address the author at zachekbooks@gmail.com.

This is a work of fiction. References to actual historical events, persons, or locations have been fictionalized. Any resemblance to other persons living or dead is unintentional.

Cover art by Carol Grant Stevens
http://www.artists-eyes.com

ISBN 978-1511813501

Acknowledgements

Thanks to my wife Amy for all your support. My deepest thanks and appreciation also go to my loyal readers Lin Courchane, Chris Schoggen, and Dan Roskom, who tirelessly pored over my manuscripts offering advice on matters large and small, and whose optimism and encouragement were tremendously gratifying.

for Mrs. Zorabel Olson,
who put up with my stories
and told me to keep at it

Preface

I call this volume *Stories from the Early Morning* because that's when I do most of my writing. Late at night, after my wife is in bed, or in the early morning, when I rise before her, seem to be the times most conducive to my muse. I often have a "four o'clock epiphany" when something I have been trying to work out suddenly comes to me.

Though I am retired, I often find the daytime hours full of distractions and seldom good for getting much writing done besides editing and polishing. But the darkness…ah, the darkness is the time when the mind roams and the imagination is kindled. It's the time when we think about where we are, where we're going, about what we've done and what might occur. It's the time when the doors open to the parallel universes from which fiction emerges.

I began writing short stories in high school, mostly hackneyed police and adventure stories about crimes, and always with fights at the end. My English teacher graciously and tirelessly read them and spent many days after school going over them with me. I am eternally grateful to her. Having been an English teacher myself, with a family and a home and a daily paperwork load, I now appreciate what a generous effort that was. I told her that my first book would be dedicated to her (it only took 53 years!).

Writing was such fun that I thought I might want to be a writer. I went into teaching partly so that I would have summers off for writing. Yeah, right. [Hence my joke at my colleagues' retirement party: If you went into teaching because you thought you would have time to write, and thirty-five years later the only nonfiction you've written is your lesson plans and the only fiction you've written is your Professional Development Plan, you might be a Retiring English Teacher!] I went nearly forty years without a single idea. How do you get ideas, anyway? Then slowly, in drips and drabs, my muse started tantalizing me with ideas, and I made the effort to pursue them.

Herewith are some of my results—some adventure, some romance, some humor, some sentiment, some nostalgia, and a touch or two of weirdness. I hope you enjoy them. Let me know what you think.

Thomas Zachek
Hubertus, WI
August, 2015
zachekbooks@gmail.com

Table of Contents

Just You Know Why

The Dave Matthews Band circulating through the surround speakers welcomed John as he pushed open the stained glass doors of the brew pub and stepped in from the cold.

The polished wood bar with its brass fixtures and gleaming trim looked particularly inviting tonight. The suspended TV screens added color to the wintry gray he had just left.

He pulled off his stocking cap and dusted the snowflakes from his wispy, graying hair, stamped the snow from his shoes, and began to unzip his down jacket. He looked around. There they were at the bar, already going at it. He could hear them over the music…

"That's easy. Woodstock!"

"No. Doesn't count. Too obvious. Something else."

He walked over to join his three friends and said, "You guys wrackin' your brains again trying to remember your youth? Didn't we do that last time?"

His friend Scott grinned, "You missed the part where we bitched about work. Now we're onto which rock 'n' roll concert you most wish you had seen. I'd vote for Beatles at Shea Stadium." He looked at the others and took a swig from his bottle of Miller.

Jeff chimed in, "Better yet—the Beatles at the Cavern or the Kaiser Klub in their early days. To see what they were like raw and raucous before they got cleaned up and pop."

"Yeah. Or how about the Monterey Pop Festival?" asked Ed.

John ordered his newest favorite beer, the house brown ale.

Scott raised his palm and added, "Or the day Dylan got electric at the—what was it?—Newport Folk Festival? Pissed off Pete Seeger and all the folkies."

"Speaking of folkies," Ed added, "How about the early days of Greenwich Village, when you could go to clubs next to each other and see guys like Dylan, and Tom Paxton, and Peter, Paul or Mary."

John took a sip of his ale. His lips came away from the glass in a wistful smile. He almost said it. Almost named the concert he now wished he had seen more than any other. But then somebody made a comment about how much concerts cost, and, as the dynamics of these conversations go, the topic switched, and he didn't feel like switching it back. Just as well. He wasn't sure he wanted to talk about it.

He spent a pleasant hour chatting and joking with these friends, and then he left and went back out to his car. But that moment in the conversation stuck with him. He could feel it coming.

He looked up for a bit at the threatening gray February sky and bundled up his coat. Snowing and cold. Again.

He drove back to his condominium. His wife of twenty-five years was not home yet, but he knew she would be in an hour or two. He also knew he had to get ready for his daughter, who was coming to visit later. But he brushed those details out of his mind for a moment. He went—he had to go—to his music shelf.

He looked around, then frowned. Where was it? The Greatest Hits CD. The purple and black one. He knew he had it here. It wasn't that long ago that he had seen it. He fumbled through his plastic CD cases…was it in the car? No, he hadn't listened to it for a long time. He shuffled through the first shelf of disks, then the second. There it was! He pulled it out and examined the cover. He stared at the smiling face, the black horn-rimmed glasses. He didn't even need to survey the list of titles for his mind to begin reeling back…

It was 1958. Early December, probably. It was cold that winter in Green Bay, Wisconsin. The wind howled through the dry tree branches on many a night, and crusted snow and ice still clung to the roads long after the last snowfall.

He was nineteen, in his second year at the University of Wisconsin Center, planning to go on to Madison the following fall. But the future was the last thing on his mind that night. Cold though it was, he was having ice cream at The Dairy Bar. Who else had been there…? Yes, Paul and David. His two buddies since grade school.

He remembered the Elvis song throbbing from the large bass speaker in the bottom section of the gleaming red and chrome Wurlitzer in the corner:

> *Won't you wear my ring*
> *Up around your neck*
> *And tell the world*
> *I'm yours by heck*

They were sitting in a booth, as they so often were, eating and playing music. Or talking about music. Or arguing about music. Or drumming with their hands on the speckled Formica counter top.

One or the other of them was picking the next song from the Seeburg selection box at the booth, always flipping through the worn red metal tabs and sliding them around their semicircular track from one side to the other, like opening so many mechanical pages in a chrome book.

"I never understood that song," Paul said. "I kept imagining a guy with a big metal ring, you know, wrapped around his neck." He kept slurping his chocolate malt in the tall, heavy, ridged glass.

"It means wear my school ring, or fraternity ring, on a necklace," David explained.

"Yeah, I know. Now."

"They have a lotta the same tunes they've had for years," John complained to no one in particular.

"Yeah, they need some new ones," Paul agreed. "Look at this—'Tennessee Waltz.' Been there forever. And Johnny Mathis? Come on. Perry Como? 'Catch a Falling Star?' And Dean Martin still with the pizza in his eye? Please. They need more rock and roll."

John said, "Well, old people come in here, too," to which they all scowled. "But they've got rock and roll. Look over here." He flipped to a later section of pages. "Here's Chuck Berry. That's a little better."

"Got a dime?" Paul asked. "Stick him on."

"'Blueberry Hill,'" John read. "Great piano."

"You want great piano?" David chimed in. "How about Jerry Lee Lewis?"

Paul flipped through selections for a while, then changed the subject: "OK—here we go. Question for the day. Best doowop group—Platters? The Del Vikings? Drifters?"

"No contest," said David. "The Drifters. You kiddin'? 'Up on the Roof!?'"

"The Platters do 'Twilight Time,'" John chimed in.

David mimed a yawn.

Paul cut in, "No—forget 'Twilight.' Best doowop song— no contest— 'Goodnight Sweetheart.' The Spaniels. Classic. Best of the Best." They leaped up and started to sing the bass intro, followed by a rather horrendously off key attempt at the opening vocal.

In the midst of these antics a girl walked in. She pulled off her wool cap to reveal her auburn hair, short-cropped. She had a rounded face and expressive green eyes and rather full lips that easily curled up into a smile when she heard the tail end of their rendition, which they cut short when they saw they were being watched. Hanging her coat up on the hook, she walked past the counter with its chrome-lined stools over to their booth.

John scrambled to recognize her as she greeted, "Hi, you guys."

"Cindy, right?" John ventured.

"Yeah. John, right?"

"Yeah," John smiled. "You're in my chem class. How'd you like that lab yesterday?"

"I got it done in time, but it was a killer," she grinned.

"Do you come here often?" John asked, and then rolled his eyes in mock embarrassment. "Oh, God, I actually said that."

She chuckled. "No. Once in a while. But I do like ice cream. What're you guys having?"

John looked down at his sundae dish and gestured with mock flamboyance. "One of my favorites—mint with hot fudge. You gotta try it."

"Sounds great."

Paul added, "It's not what he really wants, though.   What he really wants is a Pig's Dinner."

"A what?"

"Over there, on the sign."   Next to the huge red circle with the Coca Cola logo and the apple-cheeked girls raising their etched Coke glasses was a poster board whose brightly-painted, shadowed letters proclaimed, "Try a Pig's Dinner!"   The picture displayed a trough-shaped wooden dish filled with a split banana, three different flavors of scooped ice cream, three different toppings, a sprinkling of nuts and whipped cream. The tag line on the bottom exclaimed, "It's a meal in itself!"

John said, "He's bringing that up because he's too chicken to buy one. He wants me to buy one so he can share it. But I've already had one."

"You have?" Cindy asked. "What, today?"

"No, when I was in high school. I saved up my lawn mowing money. A whole seventy-five cents. My stepmom found out about it and really got mad."

She chuckled. "So, was it good?"

"Oh, yeah, it was great! But one is enough."

John slid over the red Naugahyde cushion to make room for her to sit. "So what's your favorite song?"

"Oh, I like a lot of different things. Don't really have a favorite."

She sat with them. John remembered how naturally she blended in, how much she was like one of the guys to talk to. She liked the music. She fit in.

She came in another time a week or two later.   John had arrived with Paul a little while before, and they were playing "Great Balls of Fire." He couldn't remember what foolishness they had been going on about that time.   But he remembered that he saw her drive up in the black '55 Fairlane. She had been shopping and came in with a package.

"Whatcha got?"

"The new Buddy Holly album," she grinned.

"Buddy Holly?"   John said.   "Oh, yeah. 'Peggy Sue.'   'That'll Be the Day.'   He's not bad. Catchy tunes."

Paul commented, "He's got this hiccupy voice.   As if the lyrics are being stuck in his throat."

John retorted, "Well, when you get a record contract, you can sing the songs the right way."

"Ooh, burn."

John looked at her and said, "Can I see the album?"

"Sure."   She handed it over.   He gazed at the crisp, shiny cardboard jacket bearing the photo of Buddy, a medium long shot against colored sky, standing there in his light brown suit, looking off into the distance through black horn-rimmed glasses, his broad smile like a row of piano keys.

"I'd like to listen to it.   Can I borrow it sometime?"

"Or you could buy it yourself, ya cheapskate," Paul threw in.

Rita the waitress came over and began to pick up the dishes and glassware from the next booth and stack them into her gray plastic bus tub.

Rita had worked there forever. Her ubiquitous pink dress was a bit rumpled and her frilly white collar a bit stained. She might have once worn makeup and fixed her hair to come to work, but she clearly had let those details slide as the years went on, so that now her face was lined and worn and her wispy hair a mousy brown. She remained in good cheer, however, tolerant of the much-younger crowd, trading japes with them and, every so often, letting fly with an opinion or two.

"Hey, how about putting more rock and roll on the jukebox?" Paul asked her.

"You kiddin'?" she scoffed. "The owner is thinkin' of takin' some of that stuff out."

The boys were a little shocked. "How come?"

"Customers are complaining. It's too loud, for one thing. We keep having to turn it down and they still complain. And you guys play it too much. Other people don't like it."

"But rock and roll is great. It's fun," David said.

"It's a lotta noise. And it's played by a lotta colored people. And that Elvis with his long hair and his filthy dancing. And Ricky Nelson—he was so cute and now they've got him singin' that stuff on the TV show." She cursorily finished piling up the dishes and coffee cups.

"He's still cute," Cindy said.

"Why don't you play something nicer? You know, softer," Rita said, spritzing the table top with cleaner and wiping it down. She stood up from her bus tub and looked directly at them. "Look, we like your business. You're nice boys and everything. But this music is junk. It'll never last."

"Rock and roll is OK," David offered. "There are great songs. It's getting more popular all the time."

"We just don't want a lotta punks in here," she replied, gruffly. "Don't want this place to be a hangout." She trotted off with her load of dirty dishes. John and Cindy made eye contact in bemused surprise.

John remembered leaving about the same time Cindy did, so that they walked out to the parking lot together.

"I think she's wrong about that," Cindy continued. "I think we'll enjoy rock 'n' roll music our whole lives."

It occurred to John that he hadn't thought about that sort of thing. He was impressed that she had.

They reached her black Fairlane. She pulled out her keys and began to get in. He remembered commenting, "Nice car. You like it?"

"Yeah sure, it runs great. It was my sister's. She gave it to me when she got married."

He wasn't sure whether he had said goodnight. He probably said, "Well, see ya in class."

And then there was the night of the Snow Dance, in December. He had come alone, like several of his friends, because he hadn't thought the evening would be that great, and he had been a little strapped for cash.   Such were the considerations that went into his social life in those days.

He remembered arriving about an hour after it started.   The UW Center's large multi-purpose room had been decorated with lots of tinsel and strings of lights and streams of twisted red and white crepe paper.   At one end of the room the small combo—sax, trumpet, guitar, bass, and drums— dressed in white outfits did its best to keep things lively and flowing.

He surveyed the room trying to pick out people he knew.   His eye passed over the refreshment table, and there was Cindy.   She noticed him looking, smiled, and waved.

He walked over to the table.   She was ladling paper cups half full of orange-lemon punch out of a large punch bowl, dipping her ladle down to stir up the mixture but steering around the large ring of ice floating in the center.

"Hi," he said.   "Is this stuff any good?"

"Try some." She smiled and handed him a cup. He took a sip and found it refreshing.

"So…look at you.   You're all dressed up," he said.   She did indeed look nice, he thought.   She wore a teal three-quarter length dress with a pearl necklace and a flattering touch of makeup.   Pale pink lipstick.   Even nylons with her black pumps. He had never seen her wearing nylons before. Usually penny loafers.

"And you're not so bad yourself.   Sharp suit."

"This is my funeral suit." he said, looking self-consciously at his black suit with dark red tie.

"Your what? Funeral suit?"

"Yeah, you know. The one we own for weddings and funerals."

"Well, this isn't a funeral, but it isn't much livelier."

They looked around in one of those what-do-you-say-next moments of silence. He took another sip of his punch. He watched her serve a couple who came by.

"I thought you weren't coming to the dance," John said.

"I wasn't?"

"I thought I heard you say in class that you didn't like dances."

"Well, I don't. But I'm in student government, and they're putting on the dance, so I have to help. I don't mind."

She let a moment pass, glancing at the band and back at him. "What about you? You here with somebody?"

"No, I had to work earlier. So I thought I'd come by and catch a little of it. I'm bored at home. So what don't you like about dances? Can't dance?"

"Well I can dance, sorta. But it's the music."

"What's the matter with the music?" He listened for a minute. "'Tequila.' It's a good song."

"Yeah, it's a fun instrumental and all. But I mean the songs with lyrics. They're almost all about love. And love in a sappy way. And the dances invite people to only think about the melody and the beat, and give the lyrics even less attention."

"Are lyrics supposed to be important?" John asked.

"I don't see why they can't be. Why can't people write songs about something else once in a while?"

He pondered that for a moment, draining his cup of punch.

She continued, "I mean, listen to most of the stuff this band is playing tonight. 'Fascination.' Johnny Mathis."

"They were playing 'All I Have To Do Is Dream' when I came in."

"Yeah, that's a good slow one," she allowed. "But most of this stuff is so...mushy. It's about love that, well, could never really be. It's just romantic fluff. I mean, movies can be realistic, like *Cat on a Hot Tin Roof* or *The Defiant Ones*. How come music can't be more realistic?"

"Why do lyrics have to be something to think about? Isn't music supposed to be about feeling?"

"Why can't there be some of both?"

They listened for a while. The band finished off a swinging "Tequila" and started into a soft, slow ballad with a smooth riff from the sax and the singer crooning into the microphone,

Just you know why
Why you and I
Will by and by
Know true love ways

He noticed that he had been just standing there a while, and she had been just standing there, too, and the table was lined with filled punch cups, and nobody had come up for any punch for a while, and…out it came. "So, you wanna dance one?"

She looked up at his eyes, probably a bit surprised, he thought. Then that infectious smile broke out, and she said, "Yeah, OK."

They walked to the dance floor and he took her hand, warm and a bit sweaty. They shuffled a little, then found a simple common rhythm. He looked around, a bit lost for what to do. Suddenly he realized his nose was close enough to her auburn hair to smell its fragrance. Nice. Years later he would often regret how he thought more about where to put his face or his feet than he did enjoying the moment, which lasted so briefly.

He needed to say something. "This is a nice song, even though the lyrics are about love."

"This is Buddy Holly."

"He did this?"

"Yeah."

"Not bad. Nice and sweet. Does he hiccup when he does this one, too?"

She poked him good naturedly. "No."

He tuned in to the words of the next verse:

Throughout the day
our true love ways
will bring us joys to share
with those who really care…
Sometimes we'll sigh, sometimes we'll cry,
And we'll know why just you and I know true love
ways.

Winter break came and went, 1959 arrived, and in January classes resumed. He didn't see her for a while, except in chemistry class and occasionally in the halls. She was always cheerful and upbeat. Except for one day, while he was sitting in the student lounge reading and sipping coffee. She appeared at the far entrance, looked around, and then, to his surprise, crossed the room, navigating between the tables and chairs, to his spot.

"Dang it! I'm so mad!" she said, flinging down her books.

"Hi," he said. "What?"

"The Buddy Holly tickets are all sold out!"

"Buddy Holly tickets?"

"Yeah. At the Riverside. The Winter Dance Party? February first?"

"Oh. Yeah, I heard about that. I guess it would be fun to go. But I have to work."

She looked at him, a little perplexed. "You guess it would be fun? It'll be great. Green Bay doesn't get that many stars."

"You call them stars? Most of them are up and coming, at best. Well, maybe Dion and the Belmonts have a real hit. And isn't the Chantilly Lace guy there, too?

"Yes. The Big Bopper. And Ritchie Valens. And Buddy Holly."

"Oh, yeah. You like Buddy Holly."

"That was a little dismissive." Her brow furrowed a bit. "Yes, I'd like to see him. Say, how come you're always working every weekend?"

"I work at the Bay theater. People go to movies on the weekends. Hey, why don't you come down? I can get you free popcorn. It'll almost make up for missing Buddy."

"Yeah, right." She frowned and stared down at the Formica table top. "I think I'll stay home and feel miserable."

"Well, maybe a little Buddy concert will cheer you up."

She looked at him quizzically. He stood up, grabbed a knife from the table, held it like a microphone, and began to sing, complete with the hiccupy catch in his voice:

Cindy Lou, Cindy Lou
Pretty pretty pretty little Cindy Lou
Oh, Cindy, my Cindy Lou

"My middle name isn't Lou," she said.

"Well, I didn't have a lot of time to research it."

The corners of her mouth turned up slightly. He thought maybe he had cheered her up a little. He never knew for sure. The bell rang for the next period.

February first was a busy night at the theater, for a Sunday. She never showed up, not that John expected she would.

He got off work about 9:30. The night was cold, and the heater in his Bel Air could hardly warm the car by the time he drove the eight miles home.

He turned the chrome radio knob to see what was on WDUZ. "Donna" had just finished, and the DJ said another interview with Bill Walters at the Riverside would be coming up later. He they ran an obnoxious ad for Sneezer's Snack Shop, so John punched the chrome preset tab for WBAY (with Johnny Saxe, "The Wax with the Saxe Appeal") and let Ricky Nelson ooze "Lonesome Town" from the speaker in the top center of his dashboard.

He felt really hungry, as he often did after work. A juicy burger. Yes. Maybe a malt. The Dairy Bar would be open until 10:30.

He made the slight detour to Main Street and drove on over. He turned into the parking lot, his Bel Air sliding a little on the black ice along the side of the street. He noticed that among the parked cars under the pale luminescence of the overhead lighting was the '55 black Fairlane.

He pulled open the heavy aluminum frame and glass door and stepped in from the cold. The place was not crowded. Buddy Holly was on the jukebox.

Maybe baby I'll have you
Maybe baby you'll be true
Maybe baby I'll have you for me.

Cindy was over in a corner booth dropping a quarter into the juke box selector and finishing what looked like a strawberry soda.

He walked over. "What are you doing here, drowning your sorrows?" he asked. "What happened to staying home and feeling miserable?"

She looked up and half-smiled. "I couldn't stay home tonight. I don't know. I just get the feeling that I'm missing something. I don't like to miss out."

He slid into the other side of the booth. "There'll be other concerts."

"You kidding? This is Green Bay. How often does somebody come here?"

He watched her drain her soda and listened to the song end, unsure of what to say.

"Hey, I've got an idea," she perked up. "Let's go there."

"Go where?" John asked.

"The Riverside. See what's going on. You know, just to be there." Her eyes began to gleam.

"They won't let us in," he said, wondering what she expected.

"Well, no, but I'd just like to be there anyway. Just for a while. I've got nothing better to do right now. Come on! It might be fun."

"I was gonna order. I'm hungry."

"You can eat any time. You can come back here afterwards." She waited for a moment. "So, you up for it?"

"Are we taking separate cars?"

"Sure. I'll meet you there."

The parking lot of the Riverside Ballroom was only about two miles down the road. He followed her down Main Street past the rows of red brick factories and store fronts, until the street merged into the residential section of pre-war two-story bungalows surrounded by large trees. They turned right into the Riverside parking lot, which was framed with a canopy of tree limbs that in the summer were leafy and lush, but now were merely a tangle of branches and sticks.

The concert was well under way, of course. They found separate places to park off to the side of the lot. As they got out into the frigid night air, they noticed that the serenity of the parking lot belied the warmth and vitality of what was going on inside. About four guys were off to one side, drinking beer and laughing.

They approached the white building and could vaguely hear the music inside—first the thumping bass, then strains of vocals and a muffled roar of applause and cheering.

"Recognize the song?" he asked.

"No. Do you?"

"No. Wait. It must be Ritchie Valens. That's 'Come On, Let's Go.'"

Cindy strained to hear. "I can't really tell. Let's go around to the back. That may be closer to the stage."

They scurried around the corner toward the rear of the building, which faced the bank of the frozen East River, crusted with brown ice and surrounded by bare, spindly trees.

They thought they heard the rolling rhythm of "Teenager in Love." That must be Dion now.

"So you just wanna eavesdrop from here?" he asked.

"Yeah. Why not? There's nobody around. Let's just listen for a while."

They did. They stood there in half light of the parking lot, their breaths swirling in foggy wisps, and listened as the faint rumbling and muffled lyrics of one song after another leaked through the concrete walls.

He was not sure how long they stood there. They didn't really talk. It didn't even seem that cold. He just remembered that she smiled. At one point he looked into her eyes and thought he saw them half close. He bent down to kiss her.

He would remember the sensation for the next forty years. The soft, moist touch of her lips, the faintly cold nose, the bit of warm air she exhaled as they joined, the abrupt coolness of night air as their lips parted.

They looked at each other a moment. Her eyes were a radiant green even in the dim parking lot illumination.

"Hey, what are you guys doing out here?"

They turned to look. It was Buddy Holly. He stood there, a few feet from the backstage door, cigarette in hand.

"Um...uh... we couldn't get tickets," John stumbled, "so we're just kinda hangin' around." He couldn't believe how much he suddenly sounded like Beaver Cleaver.

"Too bad. It's a fun show. You like rock 'n' roll?"

"Oh, yeah. It's the best," Cindy said.

Buddy was tall, nearly six feet. John noticed that his hair and eyes were brown, not the black he would have expected from his photos. His black-rimmed glasses were there, just as they should be. Buddy's voice was soft and mellow, with a bit of a

Texas lilt. His face was tanned, deeper than anyone's in Green Bay.

He took a drag from his cigarette, then blew the smoke out, looking away, and then turned to them as if he were talking to friends, companions, just passing the time. "It gets really cold up here. Is every winter like this? How do you guys stand it?"

"Yeah," Cindy chuckled. "I guess we get used to it."

"So you couldn't get tickets, huh?"

"No. Sold out," John said.

"Tell you what…." Buddy reached into his coat pocket and pulled out a sheaf of small white pieces of cardboard. "Here. We're doing a show tomorrow night in Iowa. Place called Clear Lake. It was a last-minute pencil-in on the tour. They're probably not sold out. My manager saves a certain number of these promotional tickets." He peeled off two and handed them to Cindy. Two crisp white tickets, only slightly bent, reading *Winter Dance Party 1959* and below that *The Surf, Clear Lake, Iowa.* Cindy stared at them for a moment. She looked up, into John's eyes, with an eager, enthusiastic look and a bright smile, her green eyes flashing.

"Can you guys drive to Iowa by tomorrow night? If our damn old bus can, you can. Prob'ly nobody'll get these otherwise. Wanna go?"

They looked at each other. Cindy's eyebrows rose and she smiled at John and then at Buddy. "Wow … thanks." Buddy smiled, flashing a straight row of pearly teeth.

"Buddy," somebody called from the doorway. "We're on."

"Yeah, OK." He flicked his cigarette to the asphalt and ground it out with his polished shoe. "It's time. Gotta go make the music. Maybe I'll see ya tomorrow night?"

He turned to walk through the stage door, and he was gone.

They stood silently for a moment, which led to several more, as they listened, straining to recognize what they heard inside. The bitter cold was working its way through their coats.

At length, Cindy said, "Well?" and looked at John.

"Well, what?"

"Well, you wanna go?"

"You mean for real?" he asked, apparently appearing more befuddled than he wished to.

"Yeah. How long would it take to get to Iowa?"

"I dunno…Minneapolis is four or five hours, and it's south of that. I'm guessing six or seven hours."

"So?" She was animated. "We can make that."

"We?"

"Yeah. We get up early and head out— make a day of it. We can take my car if you don't wanna take yours. Gimme something for gas."

He looked at her. "You're serious."

"Yes. Don't you think it's a good idea?"

He didn't know how to respond. He stumbled, "...Well, for one thing, tomorrow's Monday, and we have classes...."

"Oh, come on! You can cut once in a while. We can be back by Tuesday!"

"How do you figure? Drive back all night?"

"We'll work it out. Maybe we cut class two days."

"Well...I don't know if I want to cut two days. And I have to work Tuesday."

"How often do you ever get to do anything like this?"

"Like what? Take off for a sixteen-hour drive to do God knows what? See a concert?"

"Just for the heck of it. Have you ever done anything just for the heck of it? This is gonna be a fun show. You'll talk about seeing this show for years."

"Well, I just don't know," he hesitated.

"Hey, I thought we had something. I don't know, maybe I was foolish, but I thought we kinda clicked. Had a spark. You know, just the way we talked, and liking the same music and all."

"Well, we do," he said. "I'm just not sure that taking off from all our obligations for a whole day and night in the middle of winter is such a bright idea. Things could happen."

"Yeah, we could have fun."

"Well, it might be fun, yeah, but it's a long way. And the roads are icy. A lot can happen."

She pulled back from him. Her eyes narrowed, the sparkle grown dim. "You're a stick in the mud! You know what? I'm gonna go. With you or without you. I've got my ticket and you've got yours. I'm leaving tomorrow morning at 8. You got till then to decide. Unless you've already decided. You can do what you want. Go have a Pig's Dinner with Paul and David! Maybe you can make a decision on that!"

She whirled around and stomped off to her car, got in, and slammed the door. The black Fairlane roared to life and, with a bit of a squeal, careened out of the parking lot and toward the driveway onto Main Street.

The words, "Cindy! Wait!" never got out of his throat. What happened next would also be burned into his memory, relived again and again over the decades.

She pulled out of the crowded parking lot onto slick Main Street too fast, without looking. The Chevy station wagon coming from the left screeched its brakes, hit a patch of ice, and slammed headlong into her side.

The huge crash split the night. The impact pushed both cars ten feet down the street, crumpling them into twisted hulks of metal and shards of broken glass.

John just stood there, in shock, hardly hearing the screams of onlookers, hardly smelling the reek of burnt rubber and dripping gasoline.

By Tuesday evening the papers were filled with accounts of the plane crash. Buddy Holly, The Big Bopper, Ritchie Valens, and their pilot had gone down in that snowy Iowa corn field after the

Clear Lake concert. Cindy's crash occupied a small paragraph on page fourteen of the Green Bay *Press-Gazette*.

In the weeks and months after, DJ's and fans and editorialists speculated and pontificated about the meaning of that night. Some would call it the Day the Music Died. Of course, that was hardly true. The music went on. Life went on. But yet, it was never quite the same after that, John came to feel. Neither music nor life. And despite all the analysis and emotion about that night and that time, they would never quite get it right, John thought. Not four but five people died in a hulk of twisted metal on that tour. Five victims of weather, of impulse, of sudden and rash decisions. Five victims of rock and roll.

He left for the University of Wisconsin at Madison the following fall and never returned to Green Bay, except for his stepmother's funeral two years later and the occasional high school reunion, mostly to keep track of how fat and bald Paul was getting.

As the years passed, the sights, sounds and sensations of that night became part of his inner life. Sometimes they vanished for months as the pressures and distractions of college, work, marriage, or parenthood dominated, but then suddenly they would intrude at the oddest moment or the slightest provocation—a chance song on the radio, a patch of ice on the road, even the taste of ice cream.

It had happened often on nights like this, when the memories just suddenly flooded back, distant but never dimmed.

And always there in the background at these odd moments were the questions:
What if he had not stopped after work and run into her that night? What if he had not said what he said? How else might the conversation have gone? What if Buddy had not given them those tickets? And—especially—what if he had just agreed to go to Clear Lake? How might his life have been different?

These questions ran through his mind again tonight in the living room of his condominium, so that once again he was caught up in visualizing alternate scenarios in spinning, dizzying eddies of memory and speculation and outright fantasy.

He stared again at the nearly black CD cover with the subdued purple image of the smiling Buddy Holly. It was too ghostly and specter-like for him. He set it down. Not the CD. Not tonight. He turned to his shelf of vinyl LP's, passing his hand lightly over the row to one particular section, a section he turned to very seldom lately but whose contents he knew well enough. He pulled out an old worn album, the cardboard corners rounded and fanned out, the colors on the cover scuffed to creamy splotches. But Buddy's smile stared out from this one, too—still standing against the sky, in his light brown suit, still looking off into the distance through black horn-rimmed glasses, still grinning his piano-key grin.

From inside the sleeve he pulled out the bent white cardboard ticket that still read *Winter Dance Party 1959.* He looked at the ticket, which he had never told anyone about. How many times he could have shown it off, boastfully. He could have sold it (for quite a lot, he guessed). But he never did, because that would have required the painful explanation of how he got it and why it was never used.

He set aside the ticket. He tipped the black vinyl disk out of the sleeve and into his right hand, grasping it with his fingers under the center label and his thumb on the edge, careful not to touch the grooves. Laying the sleeve aside, he held the record between his two open hands and laid it onto the turntable. He pressed *phono* on the receiver and then moved the needle arm over the outer edge and nudged forward the lever to allow the arm to gently drop into place.

He sat down in the leather recliner. The turntable arm sank lightly onto the spinning disk and touched down with a subdued *whoom* as the needle sought and found the first groove. The JBL speakers crackled with surface noise for a moment, and then came the strains of Buddy's guitar, and he sang, once again,

That'll be the day
When you say goodbye
That'll be the day when you make me cry
You say you're gonna leave; you know it's a lie
Cause that'll be the day when I die.

And the tears came. A few of them fell onto the album cover in his lap, adding more splotches to those already there.

Afterword to "Just You Know Why"

This story, my first, was concocted in late February or early March 2005, and finished in May 2005, though I tinkered with it on and off after that.

The story is fiction, but based on reality. Buddy Holly did, indeed, play the second-last concert of the ill-fated Winter Tour at the Riverside Ballroom in Green Bay, Wisconsin, on February 1, 1959, and then went on the next night to play Clear Lake, Iowa. I found web sites with photos from the evening and other details. The details of the setting (Riverside, UW Center, WBAY, Bay Theater) are real. The Dairy Bar is patterned after Dehn's ice cream parlor in Green Bay, which actually does serve Pig's Dinners. Two of my friends in the 1950's were named Paul and David.

I am not John. I did not go to the concert. I lived about twenty minutes from the Riverside in February of 1959, but I was eleven years old, and never heard about all this until much later. Who knew? (My cousin went to the concert, but mostly stayed in the parking lot drinking beer and trying to pick up girls.)

I've always been fascinated by the vortex of that moment in rock history. The first wave of mortality struck that exciting, new musical genre. It came when rock had begun to get exciting, but had not yet had a chance to mature. Heaps of significance have been laid upon it (calling it The Day the Music Died, etc.). I am struck by the odd string of coincidences that preceded the choice the three stars made to board that plane—the bad weather, the bus with the broken heater, the coin toss. Who knows how things might have been different had any one of those factors not come into play?

It made me think about how many choices we make in our lives and how great directions in our lives are sometimes determined seemingly by the smallest of choices. I wanted to do a story that somehow swirled around that vortex.

I spent a lot of time listening to 50's music during the time I worked on this story, thanks to the Rhapsody web site. Re-watched *The Buddy Holly Story* and *American Graffiti* and everything. I wanted to write a story with a soundtrack (I don't know how you do that, except to refer to songs).

It's probably not all that original. Just my variation on a theme. Garrison Keillor told a terrific tale on *A Prairie Home Companion* years ago about a group of teenagers who made a road trip pilgrimage to the crash site. I am influenced by my friend Susan Urban's song "Electric Theater," which is about a girl who falls in love with a boy and loses him in a car crash, set in the late Sixties and laced with references to music from that era.

I am also influenced by the simple fact that every February I manage to think about that fateful night so long ago. Moreover, I am influenced by how indelible some moments in our lives are and how easy it is to jump back thirty or forty years ago in time, to recall how things looked or sounded or what was said. We probably all have objects in our house—photos, albums, books, whatever—that trigger instant nostalgia. It is remarkably easy to push aside all the things we think about and fret over on a daily basis and suddenly indulge in a wave of flashbacks. It can happen at any moment, set off by the smallest thing. And the music we grew up with is no small thing.

AL'S BARBECUE

My uncle Al Nelson loved barbecue. I have to start with that. He loved barbecue so much that it became his life's passion to turn on everybody to the joys of slow-cooked meat.

That passion meant several things. For one, it meant that he ran a barbecue restaurant and labored long and hard in it every week of the year. Now you have to understand that Al was Norwegian, and he grew up in northern Wisconsin, not Kentucky or Tennessee. So he was raised on lutefisk and lefse and pickled herring and bland meatballs in brown gravy and Jell-O with fruit suspended in it, which they called salad.

And when he opened Al's Barbecue Restaurant in 1980 in Eau Claire, Wisconsin, its chief competition was supper clubs, drive-ins, and one Chinese place. To people in Eau Claire, the only thing you cooked over coals was brats or steaks, and the only steak joints that served "ribs" (he always put the air quotes around them) steamed them and then grilled them at the last minute or just baked them dry in a too-hot oven. Don't get him started on that, because on that subject this normally soft-spoken man would chew your ear off. It was one of the few things he'd curse about. He couldn't stand the idea of ruining perfectly good meat with inferior cooking.

Despite all the meat he sampled, Al was slight of build, with a shock of white hair. He was kindly and gregarious, especially as he got older, and he loved to go on and on about barbecuing to anybody who'd listen. When a reporter for the local paper came to the restaurant once to interview him, he bent her ear for an hour pontificating about how barbecue is properly done: long, slow cooking over hickory at 180°, seasoning rub, mopping sauce, homemade barbecue sauce added for no more than the last 15 minutes. He gave her a plate of his ribs and brisket with a beer and took pains to point out what to look for, smell for, taste for. He pointed out, in case she didn't notice, that he had no old plows or license plates hanging on his walls, but rather a deep burgundy carpet, complementary wall covering and drapery, and white linen tablecloths topped with Plexiglas. He played soft jazz in the background, not some twangy country.

I'll never forget the look on his face when the reporter's article appeared two weeks later. He flipped through the paper (as he had been doing every day) until he found it, and saw that it was not a feature article on his place, but just a rundown of the local dining establishments with brief descriptions of each. Under his place, all it said was:

And if your tastes run to old-school, there is always Al's Barbecue Restaurant, where the meat is smoked, the cholesterol count is up there, and the clientele tends toward gray hair and polyester.

Uncle Al looked up and then looked back down at the article again. "That's it? All that time spent with her and this is all she said?" He moped around for a week after that.

But I'm getting off the track. The real story is the contest. I said that Uncle Al's mission in life was to turn everybody on to good barbecue. So his interest in the Great Southern Barbecue Cookoff was no surprise.

He heard about the Barbecue Cookoff when his friend Big Bill Barnett called him from Tennessee. Al and Bill had been buddies in the Army, and they kept in touch after they got out. When his hitch ended, Bill got a job at a local barbecue shack, and now he owns the place and still, according to Al, turns out some of the best ribs on God's green Earth.

When they managed to get together for the first time in about five years after they left the service, they discovered that they shared a love for barbecue and began trading recipes and tips. It was Big Bill who talked Uncle Al into opening a barbecue restaurant in the first place. He wanted Al to come to Tennessee and work with him, but Al wanted to stay up North. So Bill told him that if there's anything that us Yankees up North needed, it was a good barbecue place.

Bill kept encouraging Uncle Al, even to the point of sending him management tips and equipment catalogues. When a local pizzeria went belly-up and became available cheap, Al took the plunge and bought the place, inviting Bill to come up for a week to help him get started. He did, and that week turned into three weeks of laughing and reminiscing and carousing, though I think that somewhere along the line they actually did get some restaurant business talked about, because Al's been doing all right with the place ever since, and nearly everybody raves about his barbecue.

These two old friends visited each other's places and kept in touch over the years. I'd known Bill my whole life. Even though my name is Melissa, he calls me Missy, which is what I called myself when I was little. And when I tried to say "Big Bill" when I was little, it came out "Bubba," which Bill laughed at but Uncle Al told me not to say because he thought it was a Southern stereotype. When my mom, Al's sister, died when I was thirteen and Al took me in, Bill told me that if I didn't like living and working at Al's, I could come down to Tennessee with him. He meant it, too. It's like I have two uncles, both with barbecue sauce in their blood.

Bill had told my uncle about the annual Great Southern Barbecue Cookoff before, and Al had even gone once or twice, but never entered, because it had only been open to cooks in Southern states. But Bill called to tell us that this year they were opening it up to cooks from Northern states. "They must think they need t' whoop Yankee ass at somethin'!" he said.

Uncle Al put him on speaker phone so I could hear, too. "You gotta come," Bill said.

"Why do I have to come?"

"B'cawz your brisket is the best I ever ate. You have a real chance of winnin'. Your ribs are good, too, though I think mine're better," Bill allowed.

"Don't be so sure about that," Uncle Al shot back. "You're asking me to go head to head with you, you old rebel! How much did you say the prize money was?"

You could almost hear Bill's grin on the other end of the phone. "Does that mean you're comin'? Bring that sweet niece a yours, too! It'll be fun!"

Al allowed as how it might be. So Bill sent him the rules and an entry blank. Now this contest had so many rules that it took three pages to list them all. The whole thing was held in an enclosed compound where everybody had to stay, either in rented camper trailers or their own RV's. The only meats allowed were baby back ribs, pork shoulder, beef brisket, and chicken. Nobody could check in more than 72 hours in advance, and all meat had to be inspected upon check-in to make sure that it had not been pre-cooked, pre-seasoned, or marinated. All cooking had to be done on the grounds, and inspectors came around periodically to make sure of that.

So we packed up our chef's toques and our spices and our best flash-frozen cuts of Wisconsin corn-fed beef and headed down to Tennessee. Bill had reserved one of the rental trailers for us to stay in. It was a modest 20-foot travel trailer parked among a cluster of them on one end of the converted racetrack that was being used for the event. Farther down was another section of trailers where Bill would be bivouacked. Uncle Al said we'd wander over there when we finished unpacking and setting up, but it wasn't long before I heard that familiar bellow, "Is that my Missy!? Come here, Sweetie!"

I turned to see big, burly Bill Barnett standing a dozen yards away in his flannel work shirt and denims, his jowly face beaming and his arms outstretched. He ran toward me and clapped me with the biggest bear hug I could ever ask for, and for a moment I felt like I was fifteen again, and I loved it.

"How're ya doin', you ol' Yankee?" Bill said to Uncle Al. "You ready for some serious cookin'?"

"Bring it on," Al smiled. "We may just show you rebs a thing or two."

"You'll like it here. Everybody's real nice. How d'ya like the accommodations?"

We walked back to the awning that stretched the length of the trailer and looked over the stainless steel array of grill and gas burners and work area that had been assembled under the awning. Because of the inevitable smoke, nearly all the contest cooking was done outside, though the trailer did have a galley inside and a good-sized fridge.

"Think this work station'll do? I couldn't get us spots together cuz you signed up later."

"I think so, sure. Thanks for arranging this for us. I suppose you brought your own grill unit?"
"Sure, the one I use for catering. Just hitched it up to the van. You should see the new smoker I wanna get. A guy here has one. I'll have to show you later."

"Let me know what all I owe you."

"Oh, the prize money that you claim you'll win'll take care of it just fine. My spot is number seventeen, just over there." He pointed. "When you're all unpacked, come on over. I've got lawn chairs and cold beer waitin' for ya."

He had just turned to leave when the grin dropped from his face and he said, "Oh, no."

"What?"

"It's Pooper Sniffer. One a the judges. He's back again this year."

"Who?" I said.

"His name's Rupert Sanford," Bill explained. "I call him Pooper Sniffer."

"Why?" I asked.

"'Cuz he's always got his head up his ass."

If there was anybody who looked like the antithesis of a barbecue lover, it was Rupert Sanford. He was tall and lanky, with an angular, bony face. He looked like a New England postmaster whose favorite meal would be boiled beef and potatoes. He approached our site carrying a clipboard and decked out in his official-looking white lab coat with his name tag and two pens and a thermometer in his breast pocket.

He introduced himself, and as we greeted him, he promptly said, "I trust you've read and understand all the rules, gentlemen?"

Bill and Al nodded. Al said, "Oh, yes."

Sanford continued, "All meats must be inspected and inventoried. Anyone using ineligible meats will be disqualified. All cooking must be done on the grounds, and no cooking may be started before tomorrow morning. Anyone not observing the proper timelines will be disqualified. And, of course, we expect you to follow proper procedures of sanitation and cleanliness. Anyone disqualified from an event will be barred from competition for a year."

I could see what Bill meant about his tone. There was something about the way he kept saying "disqualified." As if his day wouldn't be complete unless somebody was.

"And contestants should be wearing their name tags at all times on the grounds."

"Well, yeah, OK," Uncle Al said hesitantly. "We just got here."

Bill stood up a little taller and said, "Y'know, you act like you're the hall monitor at school. I've been cookin' barbecue for twenty-five years, and whether or not I win, I don't come here jus' to follow *rules*. I come here to have a good time with nice people, and I jus' don't see why you can't be one of 'em, too."

"I'm sorry you feel that way. I don't mean to ruin your good time, but there are rules...." He said it sort of condescendingly, with half-closed eyes. "What did you say your name was... Barnett?"

"My friends call me Big Bill."

"Well, Mr. Barnett, I hope your entries taste good." He didn't have to add, but we could hear him thinking, "They'll have to."

As he walked away out of earshot, Bill said, "Y'know, I try to be as nice as I can and I think I get along with most people, but he just rubs me the wrong way."

"Forget it," Al said. "At least you know that if he picks your stuff, you won it fair and square."

"I s'pose. Hey, we're gonna be doin' enough cookin' in the next two days. How about goin' out for supper tonight? Let's see what this town has to offer."

"What you got in mind?" asked Al.

"Barbecue, o'course!"

About six, Bill drove over from his spot to pick us up. As we got into his van, I noticed the coolers filled with his iced meats into the back.

When I asked him why he couldn't just leave them locked in his trailer, he said, "Jus' cuz you can't trust everybody. I always want to know where they are."

We left the encampment and drove about five miles to a franchise place that called itself a roadhouse, though it was situated at the edge of a mall parking lot.

We pulled open the polished wooden corral-like door with the simulated wrought iron handle and stepped in. The place was large, crowded, and raucous. Neon beer logos dotted the knotty-pine walls along with lariats, branding irons, and prints of mountain landscapes. Tim McGraw's singing and pounding drum beat blared through twenty speakers.

There was a wait for a table, but room at the bar. Bill said he was thirsty (no surprise) so we were led through a maze of booths and tables to the bar, our shoes crunching peanut shells on the floor the whole way. A mounted cow skull peered down over us.

"It's pretty loud," I commented as we sat on the stools.

"Yeah, why do they want that?" Al said. "Look at how this place is set up. Hard wood floors, tall ceilings, and look at all the ductwork and pipes up there. Nothing to soak up noise. It's like they want it to be loud. And why do they need twelve TV sets on? Nobody's watching. Couldn't hear it if you wanted to."

A friendly bartender in Van Dyke beard and baseball cap greeted us, "Evening, folks. What can

I get you?"   Bill took his favorite, Lynchburg Lemonade, while Uncle Al took a beer and I ordered a daiquiri.

A waitress appeared, dressed in a short-sleeved gingham shirt gathered at the midriff, a red and white neck kerchief, and very short denim cutoffs that squeezed her thighs. "Hi, how are you guys doin' tonight? My name is Jenny, and I'll be your server," she shouted over the din, while still managing to smile perkily. "Can I start you off with an appetizer—maybe some fried cheese curds?" We looked at each other and shook our heads, no. "How about some onion rings? Buffalo wings?" We declined those and placed our order. Predictably the guys ordered barbecue, and I took a grilled chicken salad, confident that I would be sampling the boys' ribs and brisket, too.

When Jenny left, I commented, "They have to be told no at least twice before they quit asking. Corporate instructions."

Uncle Al said, "Do all the waitresses have to look like Daisy Mae?"

"Maybe you should dress your waitresses like that," Bill chuckled.

"I'm surprised at you, Bill," Al shot back. "Look at this place. One stereotype after another. Ropes and horns on the wall. Knotty pine. My place has linen tablecloths. And I play Paul Desmond. At low volume."

"Look, they have four kinds of sauce," Bill said, indicating the box on the bar sporting napkins, salt, pepper, and four plastic squirt bottles with witch's cap tips.

"You don't need four sauces," Al groused. "If you make one or two right, that's all you need."

"Try 'em anyway," I suggested.

Uncle Al squirted a dab of each one in turn on his spoon and sampled them. "This one's like mine, only not as savory," he said of the first. He dismissed the next two as slight variations on a theme. "If they want a second choice different than their basic one, they should do a Carolina-style vinegar sauce," he lectured.

"Look at this one—Satan's Sauce?" Bill noted.

Al sampled it and winced. "Tastes like ketchup with cayenne added," he said. What's the point to it?"

The talk drifted to the coming contest, until our food arrived. "Here you go, guys," Jenny said, delivering steaming platters.

"How do you like being called a guy?" Bill said to me after Jenny left.

"I don't do that to my female customers," I retorted.

Al looked at the combination plate he had been served. It was certainly large. Next to a generous portion of sauced ribs he saw a fan of evenly arranged slices of brisket, sauce drizzled over them, and accompanied by a ramekin of dark red baked beans. Occupying nearly half the platter was a huge baked sweet potato, sliced open, slathered with melting butter and brown sugar.

"This sweet potato is way too big," was Al's first comment. "It's ridiculous. Do they expect people to finish it? They'll just end up throwing a lot away."

The two of them shifted into full restaurant-analysis mode. They nibbled and poked and prodded at their meat, like detectives examining clues.

"Somethin' wrong with the food, gentlemen?" the bartender asked.

"No, it's fine," Uncle Al said, being polite.

"It just ain't barbecue," muttered Bill.

"Oh?"

"Look at these ribs," Bill went on. I looked up at the cow skull.

"What about 'em?" the bartender asked, nicely.

"They're brown."

"Aren't they done?"

"They were baked in an oven. Or maybe steamed, with a little liquid smoke, and then baked. And tossed on a hot grill at the last minute to finish."

"Yeah, I guess that's how they cook 'em. They're falling-off-the-bone tender. What's the problem?"

"They're not barbecued, son," Bill said, probably trying not to be condescending. "Barbecue means slow cooking over a low fire. The meat should be pink from the smoke, with just a little char at the edge. And there should be a little chew to 'em."

Uncle Al chimed in, "And this brisket isn't slow-cooked. It's chemically tenderized. You can taste it."

I thought the guy was going to get huffy, but no. He just smiled and said, "Well, I don't do the cookin', but I'll tell ya what. I'll be happy to give you another round on the house, if that'll make things any better."

I think Uncle Al was about to say, "No, it won't," when Big Bill piped in, "Why sure, son, that'd be real nice. I'll have me another one a these Lynchburg Lemonades, and put some Jack in it this time." Uncle Al took another beer, and when he asked me what I'd like, I just took a diet soda, figuring the odds were good that I was going to end up driving the boys back.

Sure enough, the second round merged into a third, and a fourth, and those two got to talking and carrying on about all sorts of things—how to cook, running a restaurant, the Army days, the state of the world. I got a little worried when the talk rolled around to who was the better chef.

Big Bill began to pontificate, "Y'know, what bothers me most is that this was a nice cut of meat. Look at all the meat between them bones. And very little fat. It wouldn'ta been that hard to barbecue this piece right." He took a sip of his drink and added, "Barbecuing a good cut a meat ain't that hard. The real trick is to barbecue a bad cut a meat."

"Whaddya mean?" Al asked. Where was Bill going with this?

"I mean takin' a scrawny, no-good piecea meat that nobody'd want fried or baked, and season it and flavor it and cook it carefully so that it comes out real good. That's how the slaves figured out how to cook ribs that the white master threw out after butcherin' the hog. That takes an artist."

"You mean, like you?"

"No, dummy, I mean like you! You have the skill, my friend. I bet you could take the mangiest, ugliest cut of meat and marinate it and slow cook it and do it up right!" Bill was really feeling his oats now. And I worried about the way Uncle Al was responding, as if he was starting to believe this.

"And what's more," Bill went on, "I bet you could fool that bug-up-his-ass piece-a-shit judge Sniffer, too!"

"I wouldn't want to."

"You could," Bill asserted with his broad Tennessee grin. "And I'd put money on it!"

Uncle Al took another sip. "Well, I'm sure glad I don't happen to have any scrawny old meat with me to embarrass myself by proving you wrong with," he said, muddling his diction as well as his syntax.

As they shuffled and wobbled out of the restaurant, I said, "Well, we'll never be welcome in that place again!" only half kidding.

"Aw, hell," Bill said, "if they're gonna put the word 'barbecue' on their menu, they damn well better not be afraid of somebody who knows the real thing!"

Bill didn't protest when I said I'd better do the driving. I managed to get the two of them plopped into their seats and buckled up, and I pulled out of the parking lot and out onto the highway.

It was pretty quiet in the van as I headed down the road. In the back seat, Bill was drowsily humming some country song. I glanced over next to me at Uncle Al to see if he was still awake. He was, and looked over at me, eyes half closed, and smiled. He had had a good time.

My eyes were only off the road for a second looking at him when I heard a thump, and the right rear side of the car jumped a little.

"Oh God. I think I hit something."

"There's nobody around," Bill said.

Nevertheless, I pulled the van over to the side of the road, got out, and went back to look. A few yards behind me on the pavement lay a full-grown raccoon, twitching in its death throes.

"Aww, no," I almost cried. Uncle Al and Bill both got out and came back to look at it, Bill staggering and steadying himself on the side panel of the van.

"There's nothin' you can do about it," he said. "He'll be dead in a minute. Jus' get back in and let's go."

I got back into the driver's seat, waiting for Uncle Al to buckle in, and the next thing I knew the back lift gate was open, and Bill seemed to be rooting around in one of his coolers back there.

"What are you doing, Bill? Let's go."

"Just gimme a second."

When he got back into his seat, I asked, "What were you doing?"

"Nothin'," he said. "Let's get back."

Uncle Al and I both woke up the next morning later than we expected. He rose with a start and jumped out of his bunk, hurriedly dressed, and scrambled to the kitchen and began amassing ingredients and carrying them outside to the work area, saying, "I gotta get the marinade going for my brisket!"

He busied himself with his brisket preparations while I dressed and got some breakfast. When I stepped out of the trailer, I heard a cheery, "Mornin', sunshine!" It was Bill, bright-eyed and chipper, grinning that infectious, toothy grin of his. He was sporting his white chef's coat with "Big Bill" embroidered on the breast, and carrying a little portable six-pack-sized plastic cooler. He added, "Here, Al. I got somethin' for ya."

He placed the cooler down on the work table, removed the lid, and reached in among the ice to retrieve a Ziploc bag, which he opened to reveal strips and sections of moist, pale brown or beige-colored meat wrapped in plastic.

Uncle Al looked down at it and said, "Is that…is that what I think it is?"

Bill just smiled what in his neck of the woods would be called a shit-eatin' grin. "I got as much as I could off it. There was quite a bit. I boned it for ya and everything."

"Oh, no." My lip curled. "Not the raccoon meat!"

"It's still good!" he asserted. "It's been cold the whole time." Among Bill's many talents, he was a skilled butcher and an amateur taxidermist.

Uncle Al shook his head. "I don't want that."

"Sure, you do. You know you can do something with it. Here's your chance. Fifty bucks says you can do that up so good it tastes just like pulled pork! You could even enter it!"

"You can't enter that thing in the contest!" I said, incredulous.

"Maybe not, but go ahead and see what you can do with it anyway," Bill said, still grinning. "Go on. What can it hurt?"

It was at that moment that the contest officials decided to pull one of their impromptu inspections. Word quickly passed down the rows of trailers—"Inspections coming. Judges at twelve o'clock!"

Not that the contestants had anything to worry about or hide. Any of the others, that is. But we weren't quite sure what would happen if an inspector found Bill's little bag of ineligible meat, and we didn't want to risk disqualification or something to find out. And we didn't have a lot of time to think.

We looked down the row and noticed a judge approaching. But it couldn't be just any judge. No, it had to be Rupert Sanford. He was two units down from us, with his supercilious smile, poking in coolers and rooting around in freezer units and jotting notes on his ever-present clipboard.

Fortunately for us, his meticulousness gave us time to think.

"He looks in every cooler," Bill said. "Here. Take this. I can't be holding it!"

I took the baggie of meat and walked inside the trailer. As I put it in the fridge, I heard him say, "Mr. Nelson?"

He was looking over the array of seasonings and herbs Uncle Al had out on the work table. He picked up a few jars and sniffed them. He did a lot of sniffing.

"Nice day," Bill said.

"And you are...?"

"Bill Barnett."

"Oh, yes. Shouldn't you be at your unit?"

"I was just visiting my old friend. I'm goin' back there now."

"A moment. What's in your cooler?"

"Well, nothin', actually." I could see Bill's honey-smooth Southern smile through the trailer window.

Sanford removed the lid of the cooler and peered in. "You carry an empty cooler around?"

"Well, sir, the truth is I just gave my friend Al here my last Coca-Cola."

"Hmmp," Sanford mumbled. "Well, I'll see you at your unit in a moment." He turned to Uncle Al and continued, "Now, Mr. Nelson, let's look at your meats."

"Melissa, are you ready to show Mr. Sanford our meats?" Al called, to give me a heads-up that they were coming in.

In a minute he would be looking in the fridge. I had to think fast. I slipped the baggie into my carry-all purse that was lying on the dinette table and yelled, "Come on in." I quickly turned to pretend to busy myself at the counter as Uncle Al led Sanford in past the dinette and into the cramped galley area.

"Here, Uncle Al," I said. "You show him the meats and I'll just take my purse and go outside out of your way," hoping that that was enough of a hint to tip him off that I was holding the contraband.

While Uncle Al opened the fridge and let the inspector poke through the meats, I took Bill aside away from the trailer and said, "Here, take this." I slipped him the baggie discreetly.

He was about to kneel down to open his little cooler and put the meat into it when Sanford and Uncle Al opened the door to the trailer and started to come out. Bill didn't want to be seen with the meat, so he slipped it into the spacious pocket of his chef's coat.

Sanford said, "Thank you, Mr. Nelson." Turning to acknowledge Bill still standing there, he added, "I'll see you in a little while, Mr. Barnett." He turned and started to walk away, looking at Bill and me. Bill waved politely at him and smiled what might be described as a polite grimace, then started to walk the opposite way, toward his unit. He looked back over his shoulder to see that Sanford was no longer watching him, then pulled out the packet and tossed it underhand over to me, as if we were playing touch football. I snatched it and took it over around to the back of the trailer and passed it though the window to Uncle Al, who put it in the fridge.

Whew. Hope nobody saw that.

As I came back around to the front trailer area and Uncle Al emerged from inside, Bill said, "He's coming back!"

"Why?"

"I don't know!   Pass it back out the window!"

I went around to the other side of the trailer again. Al hustled inside the trailer, snatched the meat from the fridge, and passed it back out to me through the kitchen window.

A moment later at the door, Al greeted Sanford, who said, "Just a minute, I forgot to check your inventory against your original declaration."

"Is that necessary? Do you think we went out and bought extra meat?"

"It's the rules, sir. It'll just take a minute." They went inside the trailer.

I walked over to Big Bill and discreetly handed him the package and whispered, "Here. It's yours."

"No, sweetie, your uncle's gonna cook this."

"Get it out of here!" I said in an urgent whisper.

Bill started to walk away and I turned toward the trailer. At that moment Sanford and Al were just coming back outside, and Sanford was saying, "Very good, Mr. Nelson. That'll be all. See you at the judging tomorrow afternoon."

Sanford walked on, and Uncle Al turned toward the two of us standing there in the yard with an expression on his face that said subtly, yet clearly, "OK, who's got it?"

"Well, I guess everything's fine then," I said, fearing Sanford might still be within earshot.

"Oh, here, Al," Bill said, holding out the cooler. "Why don' you just fill this up with beer and bring it over after a while?"

"Uh, sure," Al said.

I took the cooler from Bill. I could tell by the weight. We were holding the road kill again.

Later that night—well past bedtime—I awoke to the sounds of Uncle Al outside bustling around the work area. I put on my robe and slippers and went outside. I found him whisking olive oil, lemon juice, balsamic vinegar, garlic, and some kind of alcohol, and he had laid out an array of spices, including cumin, celery seed, cayenne, fennel, and others I wasn't sure of. I had to admit, but didn't say, that it smelled pretty good. I just said, "What are you doing?"

"Nothin'. What're you doing up?" He blended a few spices in his hand and sniffed and tasted and added some to the bowl.

"You're making a marinade for that raccoon meat, aren't you?" I said in a more urgent whisper.

"Sshhh. Go back to bed," was his only response.

"Uncle Al! This isn't like you! You're going to get in trouble!"

He shot me a look that was the closest to impatient ire that I've ever seen in that gentle man, and waved his hand dismissively.

"It doesn't matter what Bill says," I went on. "Let him cook it if he thinks it's such a good idea!"

"Just go to bed, Melissa."

I knew there was no use lecturing him about competitiveness or health concerns or how he was wasting his time staying up late. Big Bill had pressed his buttons again.

The morning of the final judging was truly a sight. Most of the cooks got out early to fire up their grills. The smell of barbecuing meat permeated the entire compound, and hickory smoke hung heavy like an ambrosial cloud over the grounds. Ribs baked lazily in covered grills while chickens and pork roasts slowly turned on spits, sizzling and sweating oils and basting juices. I could see why barbecue chefs got enthusiastic about this competition. The excitement in the air was as palpable as the smoke. I took a walk down the rows and watched as aproned and toqued chefs slathered mopping sauce over their meats and seasoned and tasted their simmering sauces. Some of the chefs hunkered over their meats grim-faced and serious, like scientists monitoring an experiment, but most of them were a jovial lot, laughing and joshing and inviting people to sample their wares. Some offered me tastes as I walked by, and a couple even offered me a beer. At nine in the morning.

Uncle Al had been lovingly tending to his slabs of beef brisket for some time already, dabbing the mopping sauce, watching them sizzle. They smelled and looked terrific, as always.

When I returned from my stroll and saw him at work on his real meats, I said, "OK, today's the day of the final judging, and it's all over now, right? We're past that raccoon nonsense?"

He smiled what I'd call his Northern equivalent of Bill's SEG and pointed to a little section of meat slowly cooking at the rear of the grill, poking it and turning it a little.

"Huh? Uncle, Al, you're not going to…?"

"Shh, now honey, don't worry. I'm just going to cook it up and give it to Bill to taste. And that'll be the end of it. It's just a joke."

And he did. When Bill stopped by to see how things were faring, Uncle Al scooped the barbecued meat onto a Chinet plate and handed it to him with little flourish.

"Let's see what we got here," Bill said. He actually tasted it and added, "Pretty damn impressive." Then he looked at me and said, "Don't wrinkle your nose at me, sweetie. Did you try it?"

"No."

"Then maybe you don't know what you're missin'."

"Yes, I do."

"I tell you, you could enter this, Al."

"Well, I'm not," Al said. "Now get it out of here."

The judging was held late that afternoon under a large canopy at one end of the grounds. The contestants and their friends and families, hundreds of them, gathered in lawn chairs or on foot to listen to the warm-up bluegrass band. The crowd was in a festive mood, and side bets and beer flowed freely. Five hundred dollars was riding on the first place selections in each category, so there was a lot of excitement.

A portable stage had been set up bearing tables, behind which sat the panel of three judges, Sanford and two others. They were doing chicken first, then brisket, then ribs, and finally pulled pork. So many people entered ribs that they had to have an elimination round earlier in the day. "What a job, tasting ribs all day," Al commented.

Al's brisket didn't win, though it did get an Honorable Mention. He thought that was pretty good, considering the competition he'd seen. He was really proud walking up there to get that certificate he could put on his restaurant wall.

Bill's ribs passed the first round, but didn't place. He blamed it on the fourth Lynchburg Lemonade. He started to make notes about what he would do differently next year, when the pulled pork competition was announced and he snapped to attention.

People could register to enter an event as late as this morning. When they read off the list of entrants in the pork division, Uncle Al's white eyebrows arched when he heard Bill's name. He turned to Bill and said, "I thought you weren't going to enter the pork. When did you change your mind?'

"Oh, I jus' decided I had me somethin' good this year," was Bill's only reply.

The judges were served portions of the cooked meat from warming dishes that were identified only by number. A little meat from each entry was placed atop half a sandwich bun for each judge, and they each took bites in turn. Each judge awarded points, the winner being the one with the highest total.

As we stood in the crowd watching Bill's entry, which we knew as number 6, being scooped out of the pan, Al went wide-eyed and whispered, "Wait a minute. That doesn't look like your pulled pork. That looks like....."

"Shh," Bill said. "Pay attention."

Uncle Al looked at me. We traded glances that said, "Did he...? He didn't. Did he?"

We both looked back at Bill, who smiled that wicked grin of his and turned toward the stage and said, "I don't care how it goes. Either way, I jus' wanna see his face when he bites into it."

Judge Sanford held the sandwich to his nose to smell it and then jerked back just a little. Then he smelled it again and nodded. Still grim-faced, he took a small bite (he always took small bites). He chewed slowly. His expression was blank.

Then his eyes widened.

Al and Bill looked at each other. I figured this was it. He was going to spit it out any second and the jig would be up. Bill held up his hand as if to signify, "Don't worry."

At that moment the judge stopped chewing.

And a small smile came over his face. He actually said, "Interesting." And then, taking another bite, added, "Yes, really interesting. Quite a flavor."

Bill became red-faced and couldn't contain himself, bursting out chuckling, then looking down and stifling the laughter to avoid undue attention. Uncle Al just looked on, wide-eyed, and slowly shook his head.

But that wasn't the kicker. The other two judges nodded in approval, too. At the awards presentation, I couldn't believe it when they announced it—Bill won third place in the Pulled Pork Sandwich division! I also couldn't believe that Bill went through with it, walking up there with his mile-wide Tennessee grin, accepting that medal and that $100 prize check. Uncle Al, as Bill often put it later, "didn't know whether to smile, spit, or swallow!"

And that's how my uncle Al Nelson from Eau Claire, Wisconsin, won third place in the 12th annual Great Southern Barbecue Cookoff by barbecuing road kill and feeding it to the anal retentive expert judge.

He let Big Bill keep the money and the certificate, but they both know who really won and how and why. And neither one has ever told or ever will tell (unless maybe you get one of 'em really drunk). But as long as Big Bill doesn't spill the beans, the truth will be safe with me.

But I'm dreading the day when somebody dares to suggest to my uncle that some piece of meat wasn't done right. Because Al might haul off and tell him just how good he really is. Because Uncle Al loves barbecue, you know.

Afterword to "Al's Barbecue"

"Write about what you know and what you like!" they always tell you. So what do I like? Enjoying a meal at Texas Roadhouse one day, I thought, well, I really like barbecue. There aren't that many stories about barbecue. Wouldn't that be a good subject? That's what started it.

So I wrote a barbecue story by this title but wasn't pleased with it. This is the only story so far that I have completely redone after drafting it once. In the original story, there is no contest. Al dies and Melissa takes over the place. I began it with an extended interview with the reporter, where he feeds her ribs and describes in exquisite detail how they should be done. I wrote that scene, but it sat undeveloped for a year before I finished the original.

After doing several other stories, I went back to this one. I thought I had created this interesting character in love with barbecue, and then I just killed him off. I wanted it to have more— more character, more fun, more something. I thought back to some of my earlier ideas about story possibilities I had considered and rejected, and began to focus on the barbecue contest idea. How would Al get involved in that? Then I hit on the idea of an old buddy from the south who ropes him into it. OK. And I kept coming back to my opening line, which I liked, "Al Nelson loved barbecue." What might that mean, exactly? I can't have him just win the contest. Too pat. But somehow his love of barbecue has to come through. So I began to toy with where I might go with that.

I preserved some elements from the first version. Melissa is still there, but she has become his niece. And I transposed it to first person narrator. The visit to the roadhouse restaurant is still there, but I put a different spin on it and made it organic to the plot, which I think is better.

The scene at the roadhouse is based on the Texas Roadhouse chain, but I don't dislike them as much as the boys did. I also worked in some of my pet peeves about restaurants (Pizza Hut actually does instruct its servers to get two no's on appetizer offers before moving on.)

The Night Pete Seeger Came

    The heat of the spotlight spread across my face. As I built to my finish, I hoped my voice wouldn't quake.

    Last verse. So far so good:

How many times can a man turn his head

OK, now, nice and smooth from D to G to A:

and pretend that he just doesn't see?

Get ready…stretch to the B minor and punch it out:

The answer, my friend, is blowin' in the wind.

The answer is blowin' in the wind.

Smooth segue to the 7th chord, deep breath…repeat the coda:

The answer, my friend, is blowin' in the wind.
Look right at 'em...slow it down with firm strums
to bring it home...believe it!
The answer is blowin' in the wind.

The applause was decent. The crowd was
smiling. My fingertips were sore and my brow was
sweaty, but I didn't care.

I broke out of my intense, oh-so-serious-
folk-singer face and grinned at the audience and
said, "Once again, my name is Gary Wood and
thank you ladies and gentlemen, thank you again for
coming out and supporting folk music in the
Village. You're at Sal's, the home of the rising
stars on the folk music scene, with music every
Thursday through Sunday night, and poetry on
Wednesdays." I had the club-plugging patter down
so rat-a-tat-tat that I almost forgot, until my eye
caught Dan the bartender pointing toward the sign
on the wall.

"Oh, yeah, and don't forget our fantastic
talent contest next month," I added. "Five hundred
dollars first prize. And word is that none other than
Pete Seeger himself might be coming in to serve as
one of the judges. So brush up on those chords and
let's see a lot of you out there. Amateurs only, the
more the merrier. Details from Dan, our smiling
bartender, who only waters down the drinks if you
don't tip."

Dan waved from behind the bar, his smile
only slightly grimacing. OK, I needed a new line.
Better move it and get off the stage. I continued,
"And now on with the entertainment. Batting

cleanup tonight is my friend and yours, a very talented singer and a great guy. Let's give a warm welcome to our feature act, Leon Sullivan!"

The crowd applauded politely as I hopped off the stage and Leon stepped up right after me. The stage was small, rising only a few feet above the floor, and there was no wing space, so the performers generally stood around at the end of the bar, looking inconspicuous, until the moment when they ascended the stage and the spotlight drew all the attention to them.

I gratefully accepted the one free beer that Sal gave us every night after our sets. It felt good on my parched throat.

Jill Cooper came over and said "Good set tonight."

"Thanks," I replied, smiling back at her. "You had a nice set, too. Too bad about that drunk talking loud during your soft song."

"Yeah. I'm glad he left." Jill was short and slight of build, with a rounded, pleasing face, intense brown eyes, Joan Baez haircut, and pale skin that spoke of spending a lot of time indoors, partly from the New York winter and partly from hours spent practicing, like me. We were a pasty lot. She was wearing the crocheted vest that I liked, along with her dungarees and her black turtleneck. She turned and cocked her head to listen to a phrase Leon was singing on stage, commenting, "Leon's in good form tonight."

"Leon's always in good form," I replied. It was true. Leon had a strong, resonant voice, and the smooth, rich tones of his Martin guitar sounded terrific, even on Sal's sound system. From the stage I couldn't really tell how mine sounded—everybody said it sounded OK—but I knew I couldn't match his sound.

I hung around as usual until Leon's half-hour set was over, alternately watching the show and talking with Jill and Dan.

Sal was off at the other end of the bar, chatting with a couple of guys while keeping one eye on the show, more on the crowd's responses than on Leon. Sal was short and pudgy, with a ridge of graying hair circling the back of his head beneath his bald dome, and by this time of night his jowly face bristled with whiskers.

As a club, Sal's was a notch or two above a dive. It was an old place, having been a bar on that corner of the Village for decades. It was square and boxy, with creaky floors. The worn mahogany bar stretched along one side, complete with a tarnished brass foot railing straight out of the old days. The back bar had a really fancy old-style mirror about five feet high, surrounded and embellished by carved wood that still looked good today. The rest of the linoleum floor space was furnished with a motley assortment of chairs and Formica and wood tables that he had gotten second- or third-hand. The walls were lined with a few art prints and posters of upcoming area gigs.

To his credit, Sal had been trying to class up the place, slowly but surely. In the early days of the folk scene (that is, two years ago), he didn't even have a sound system, but now had worked his way up to decent mikes, amps, and spotlights. The johns were next on the list, we hoped.

And now Sal had decided to up the ante with a talent contest.

"So, is Pete Seeger really coming?" I asked him when I had a chance.

"Well, his agent said he'd be in town, and this is the kind of thing he likes to see," Sal answered, and added with a smile, "and when big names show up, you never know who else will be sniffing in the woods, like talent scouts and record executives."

Yeah, right. He wouldn't *say* that he had Pete or record executives coming around. Just hint at it. So if they didn't show up, his butt was covered. That was Sal.

My life revolved almost totally around music in a way that I had never expected even two years ago, when I moved to the Village after dropping out of NYU. I had fallen into the folk music world in high school almost accidentally when I hooked up with a bunch of other guys who played guitar and got together for jams. I started going to open mikes, and the next thing I knew I was invited to be an opening act at Sal's, at first for beer and tips, and then later for a regular slot as the middle act, for actual money.

Along the way I discovered a vast treasure of musical heritage—the Weavers, the blues, the Carter family, spirituals, and on and on. It seemed like every other week somebody was bringing in an old record he found in a second-hand shop and saying, "You gotta listen to this!"

But what was really exciting was the new talent coming in. Within nine blocks of Sal's there were at least five clubs that offered folk music, and the area had started to become a nexus that attracted talent from all over. We had troubadours and rising stars come around regularly—guys like Tom Paxton and Phil Ochs and Bob Dylan—who were even starting to get record contracts. And these guys visited each other in the clubs and hung around afterward and we got to know each other so there was this cross-pollination.

And the jams! We got together a couple nights a week after hours at one of the clubs, or maybe at somebody's pad. We sat in a circle and just played whatever we felt like playing, round-robin style. We never knew who would stop by or what he'd bring with him. This is where guys would haul out an old classic, or where somebody into blues would trot out a Robert Johnson gem that he'd discovered. Sometimes we were floored by a new song somebody was working on. Sometimes we got on a crazy roll and tried to see how many songs we could think of with the same chord progression (it always worked with Fifties' ditties like "Heart and Soul" and "Silhouettes" and "All I Have To Do Is Dream").

That was the way it went tonight. We gathered at Leon's place two blocks away, passed around some Mateus Rosé, and sang for two hours—me, Jill, Leon, plus Wes, Craig and Steve, three other guys who occasionally played with us.

Steve played mandolin, and sat in with us in our sets from time to time, playing sweet backup.

Phil Ochs came by tonight, too. He had a gig down the street and, as usual, he brought a new song or two. He already had a record contract with Elektra, but he still hung out with us and didn't rub it in or anything.

Phil was very intense, with his black, slicked-back hair and darting eyes. So different from the laid-back Tom Paxton, who also came by from time to time. Tom's songs were gentle, wistful things like "Rambling Boy." Phil's were hard-driving polemics, full of biting social commentary. He crammed a lot into four minutes.

Leon picked up these new songs like a sponge. When Phil sang his song tonight, Leon was playing along by the second verse. At the end, he said to Phil, "How does that third verse start?" as if he already remembered the first two, which he probably did. Me, I'd have to ask him to write down all the verses and work on them for two weeks to get them down. And I never really felt like doing that.

A moment came when a song ended and nobody immediately launched into another, so I asked, "Are you guys gonna enter the contest?"

Leon and a couple of the other guys said they would. I say "guys" but Jill was always included.

Phil said, "I can't, of course, because it's amateurs only, nobody with a record contract. How about you, Gary?"

"I don't know," I replied. "We get fifteen minutes, so that's like four songs. What should you try for in such a short set?"

Steve said, "Well, if Pete Seeger's gonna be there, he's gonna like something with a traditional flavor. Ideally, a political song with a singalong chorus."

Jill said, "Yeah, but if some record guy is there, he's gonna want something fresh and new, something different from what everybody else is doing."

Leon added, "We know that one of the music critics from the *Voice* will be there, and he's gonna give points for musicianship and style."

"So," I said, "what we need is original stuff that sounds traditional, brand new stuff that sounds as though we've polished it for months. Got it."

They all chuckled, and then Phil said, "Look, just be yourselves. Find your own voice. It's the only way."

Somebody started up the old "Drunken Sailor," and pretty soon we were improvising bawdy verses ("What You Gonna Do With a Drunk Folk Singer?") and polishing off the last of the Mateus.

I often left these sessions with my mind reeling from the sheer excitement of all the music that I'd been exposed to. As I headed down the street from Leon's flat to my place, the night was cold and crisp and very quiet. Hardly a light on or a car in the street. What was it, two a.m.? The late-night cold wind swirling down the streets and alleys provided a sharp contrast to the heady warmth of the jam session.

I walked past the row of familiar storefronts—the Chinese restaurant where we often got takeout, the record shop and used book store we haunted, the military surplus store where half our wardrobe came from. Passing the Village Hardware Store, I noticed once again the hand-lettered sign in their window, "Help Wanted. Days and some Eves. Apply within." That reminded me, much to my chagrin, of how short I was last month. And this month didn't look much better. Though I had a cheap flat, and didn't spend much, I wasn't making much at Sal's, either. So far I had been getting by, but I kept liking the sounds of the other guys' guitars so much, especially Leon's Martin, that I'd been increasingly dissatisfied with my own and wanted to get a better one.

The eternal triangle—food, rent, guitars. Can have one, maybe two, but can't have all three. Damn.

I walked up the dirty staircase three flights to my small apartment. It wasn't much—one main room with a sitting area on one side, kitchenette on the other, plus a small bedroom and a bath. I set my guitar case down and settled down onto the worn couch.

"Secondhand" was a polite way to describe most of my stuff: the well-used couch, the cinder-block-and-board shelves for books and records, the Formica table in the kitchenette, the Norge refrigerator, the cheap clock radio with the plastic grille.

I reached over to switch on the radio, which I kept pretty much locked onto the same station, my main source for new music outside of the club circle. That station played folk music for most of the day, sometimes including the new recordings of people I knew from the clubs. At this hour, the late-night jock was heavily into soft jazz. I listened to him long enough to catch the segue from Duke into Thelonius Monk and then hit the hay.

I spent a long time mulling over—agonizing over—what I would do for a contest set. A week after the last session, the jam was at my place. It was the usual crowd, except that Leon didn't make it, but the rest of us spent some time talking again about what we would do for our contest sets.

As we were breaking up about one, I was sorta surprised when Jill asked, "Gary, can you help me with a coupla my songs?"

"Hey, sure."

She remained after the rest left. I straightened things up a little while she tuned her guitar on the couch. She said, "I've been trying to write stuff, but whatever I think of I automatically dismiss as either too stridently political or too trite."

She sang me a few of the songs she'd been working on. They weren't bad—she had talent. I gave her what few suggestions I could think of.

I took up my guitar and we sat half-turned toward each other on the couch and spent some time working out licks and progressions.

At one point, she said, "The idea that Pete Seeger might be there makes me really nervous. He's never been in the club before, and for him to show up, even to listen, is a big deal."

"Yeah, I know. He's what this music is all about. He's the voice of this whole movement … traveling around with Woody Guthrie, marching for causes. He uses his music to change the world in ways people haven't done before."

"And yet he's this really nice guy who can charm an audience," Jill added, and then mused, "So what would he like?"

"He likes a lot of things," I answered, not very helpfully. "The question is what would he give the prize to?"

"What are you gonna do for your set?" she wondered.

I ticked off a short list of things I'd been thinking of doing, mostly songs I knew well from jams or sets. Maybe some blues, maybe some Paxton….

"Have you been writing anything?"

"Well, I wasn't gonna bring it up yet, but I'm writing a song for you."

"Me? Really?" She gazed rather sweetly at me.

"Yeah."

"Well, can I hear it?"

I hesitated. "It's not finished yet. I just have a chorus and half a verse, and I'm not even sure of the melody."

"Well, just gimme a taste of it." She put her guitar down and fixed her brown eyes on me.

So I sang what I had, my voice quavering a little. "See? Told ya it wasn't much. I gotta put a minor into it. Phil said if you want a singalong broadside, stick with major chords. But if you want to make it sweet and poignant, work in a minor."

She smiled warmly and said, "But it's nice. Nobody's ever tried to write a song for me."

"Yeah, well, it was between you and Dan, and I couldn't find much to rhyme with 'bartender,'" I said, trying to inject a joke. She chuckled.

"It's hard to write a new song," I continued. "I don't know how Leon does it. He seems to have a new song every other week. He'll probably have one for the contest."

"Yeah, I think he's working on one or two."

"My fingers are sore," I said. "Let's take a break."

I put my guitar down. She leaned back in the couch. "Thanks for helping me out," she said. "I'm still not sure what I'm going to do, but I have a lot better idea of what will work. It's nice to have a sounding board."

"And I'm glad to help," I smiled back.

I opened a bottle of Ripple I had in my fridge, and we shared some of it and talked for quite a while. We talked about a lot of things—how much we liked folk music, the people we'd gotten to meet, the power of music.

At one point, Jill leaned back, gazing off somewhere, and said, "You think about all the things going on in society today—the civil rights movement, the labor movement, all the social change—so much of it is propelled by music. It's exciting. We're at the vanguard of something here." She paused to take a sip of her wine, and added, "You know, I don't know where I'll be in ten years, but I'm sure glad I'm here now." She smiled again, serenely.

"Me, too, " I whispered. I leaned forward and kissed her. She kissed back.

Weeks passed, and the night of the contest arrived. And I was late. I don't know what happened. I had been practicing my set, and then took a little nap, thinking I had plenty of time. I went to grab a pizza for supper, and before I realized it, it was time for the contest and I was late.

I ran the two blocks to the club, my guitar case swinging back and forth. I hoped that Sal hadn't done some preliminary group intro of all the contestants or something, because then I'd be screwed if I missed that. I rushed in, but trying to be inconspicuous about it, if that's possible.

Some guy I never heard of was onstage, probably a local college kid. He was trying to do a number on Sal's old battered upright piano, which he should have assumed was not in tune. He stunk.

Geez, that was mean. I guess I was in a real piss-ant mood, for some reason. I had to get outta this funk before my turn.

I set my guitar down in the back, bought a beer from Dan, and settled in and looked around. A judges' table was set up in the back where three guys sat, note pads in front of them. I didn't really know who any of them were, having missed their introductions, too. One was tall, distinguished, with graying hair, wearing an out-of-place suit and tie. Him I pegged as the *Voice* critic. Next to him was a balding man with horn-rim glasses and a bushy mustache. The third was a fat, red-faced guy I thought I'd seen around the clubs at one time or another but never met. I figured maybe one of Sal's friends in the business.

No tall, lanky Pete Seeger. Dammit, Sal.

I heard somebody at the bar say Pete might be stopping in later. Well, maybe. I had a while before my turn.

I looked around for Jill and saw her across the room, sitting with some friends. I don't know if she saw me. I don't know if she was looking for me, either.

A few more contestants did their sets, and I half listened. I exchanged a few comments with some of the guys at the bar, while I kept glancing across to Jill. I kinda lost track of the time, until I realized that I was next after the guy who was on. And then he started doing "San Francisco Bay Blues," which was the song I was going to lead with! Sonofabitch!

I quickly ran through my mental inventory of titles that I could just stick in without rehearsing. I wanted something fun and upbeat…a Woody song? A Dylan song? Nothing came to mind. I couldn't focus. I'd just have to go with the other three.

When my turn came, I didn't get any warm, appreciative intro, just my name, said twice. In that first moment in the spotlight, I tried to read the audience and gauge whether they were just getting warmed up or had had enough, but I couldn't really tell. The three judges sat in the back, rather poker-faced. OK. So I just had to charge ahead.

I opened with the blues number I had worked up, "Keys to the Highway." Slow and expressive. I tried to wow 'em with a little guitar work, which I think I did. My fingers popped on and off the frets crisply during the turnarounds, and on the break I bent and slid the notes the way I hoped—knew—I could. So far, so good. Fingers were working better than my brain was.

For my next song, I did Tom Paxton's "I Can't Help But Wonder Where I'm Bound," one of my jam favorites. I started out just fine, nice and bouncy, but I muffed the third verse when I began singing:

> *I had a little gal one time*
> *She had lips like sherry wine*

and then I slipped into the fourth verse:

> *And I hear she's out by Frisco Bay.*

So then I was stuck and had to finish up the fourth verse to keep the rhyme scheme, trying to remember to change "him" to "her." And then I just jumped to the final verse and didn't try to salvage the third. And I probably speeded up.

Without much patter, I moved on to "This Land Is Your Land" to close. I had learned some of the lesser known, more radical verses, thinking that would have impressed Pete. It didn't matter now, but I didn't have a different finale, so I just plowed ahead with it. I did manage to get the crowd to sing along. They were polite.

A few people said, "Nice job." Everybody got told, "Nice job."

I didn't even pay attention to the guy who was up next. Somebody new. I went to the john, and then bought myself another beer and vaguely heard some lukewarm applause after his last number. And then Sal introduced Leon, who was last.

Leon bounced up onto the stage and began thrumming a hard-driving C-Em-Am-G7-C chord progression even before the applause died down, wasting no time setting up an energetic tempo. When he knew he had their attention, he launched into:

Come and take a walk with me
through this green and growin' land
Walk through the meadows and the mountains
and the sand

He was doing Phil's "Power and Glory." Great choice. Solid and invigorating.

He followed with the classic "Colorado Trail," which surprised me, because I thought it kind of old hat. But he had re-worked it, making it slow and wistful, a fresh reading of an old chestnut.

He looked good up there in the spotlight, with his firm jaw and angular cheekbones, combed but not slick black hair, soft cotton shirt, and leather vest.

As the considerable applause was just dying down, he smiled and said, "I'd like to do a new song, a song about somebody special." He called it "Angel with Both Feet on the Ground," and it was sweet and tender.

Oh, God, he was doing a song about Jill. Shit.

Even though the lyrics were not specifically about her ("vagued up," they called it), I could tell he meant her. I didn't need to see her smiling and staring dreamily at him from the audience to know. They'd been getting it on. How long, I wondered.

I couldn't really feel mad at him. Just empty. And glad I didn't have to follow him.

He introduced his fourth song by saying, "And now I'd like to end with a new song by a friend of mine named Phil Ochs, who wrote the first song. It's about his life, and I guess it's about mine, too." He took a breath, closed his eyes, and smoothly crooned, a capella:

There's no place in this world where I'll belong
When I'm gone

The gentle finger-picked guitar strings slowly came in and up as he continued :

And I won't know the right from the wrong
When I'm gone
And you won't find me singing on this song
When I'm gone
So I guess I'll have to do it while I'm here.

He cruised effortlessly through six verses and ended by repeating the first verse again, but softer, with the lightest, most delicate touch on the strings. He punched up the last line with more repetition:

I guess I'll have to do it
I guess I'll have to do it
I guess I'll have to do it...

He built up the last phrase, the guitar fell silent, and with eyes closed, impassioned, he stretched out *while I'm heeeere* until he let it fade, hanging in the air. For a moment, the place was silent and you could hear a pick drop. Then the crowd erupted in wild applause. Even Sal stood up and clapped, grinning from ear to ear.

It was a masterful set. A thoughtful blend of old and new, sweet and powerful.

Of course Leon won the contest. He'd brought the house down.

Pete Seeger never did show up. I felt like asking Sal whether there had even been a chance that he would, but thought better of it. It didn't matter. I didn't need to fall on my face in front of anybody famous.

It turned out that the balding guy with glasses was a record exec from Decca. Packing up my guitar, I saw Sal call Leon over to meet the Decca guy, who shook Leon's hand and clasped him on the shoulder as he talked. Jill wandered over, smiling, and Leon put his arm around her.

I watched Leon leave with the prize check—and Jill.

As I trudged back home down the dark streets, pulling my collar up against the cold winter wind, my mind was a swirling eddy of thoughts and feelings.

I stomped up the stairs to my walkup. Inside, I threw my guitar case down and went to the fridge to pour myself the little remaining Ripple that I had. I flopped down on my couch and stared for a long time at some crumbs on the floor. Suddenly my apartment seemed really crappy.

I had a lot of questions. Did I think Leon wouldn't win the contest? Did I think I really had a shot with Jill? What was I doing, anyway? Where was I going? Maybe this whole folk music thing wasn't for me. What, did I think I was going to change the world or something? It was just music. Words and chords, that's all. Maybe somebody's music would change the world, but not mine. Maybe I'd better get up early tomorrow and see about that hardware store job. I could still play on weekends. . . .

I switched on the radio. The DJ said, "And now let's listen to something new that just came in, something a little different. It's called...let's see...yeah, it's called 'I Want to Hold Your Hand.' Here it comes."

Afterword to "The Night Pete Seeger Came"

The title is ironic, of course. Once again, a story about music, and a story that opens in a bar (for a while there, every story I wrote seemed to involve beer). Nobody dies in this one, though.

I've long been interested in the early days of seminal movements (particularly music) and how things get started. I'd already written about the early days of rock and roll in my Buddy Holly story. It must have been exciting to be in the Cavern Club, say, to see the early Beatles perform. I read that at one point in the Fifties one could walk down the streets of Memphis and in the same night, at nearby clubs, see Elvis, Roy Orbison, Jerry Lee Lewis, and Johnny Cash all performing. And so it was with folk music. There was an incredible surge in popularity of folk music in the late Fifties and early Fifties, and the Greenwich Village scene was the vortex of that movement. Bob Dylan, Tom Paxton, Phil Ochs, Peter Paul and Mary and many others were attracted to this area and began their careers there. What must it have been like? I wrote this story before *Inside Llewyn Davis* came out, but it's the same milieu.

I'd been interested in folk music for a long time, and jammed with a lot of good folks in song circles, and the music of this period was my favorite. So I thought that this, too, must have been an exciting time, and I wanted to do a story about that. So I imagined a club and a stable of struggling young folk musicians, and I thought of working in a famous name or two and some of the songs of the period. I wanted dialogue about the power of music. I tried to convey the sense of singing and performing songs. But I couldn't just do a history of the music or the area. I needed a focus, a plot. Hence the idea of a struggling, middling folk singer in a club, and the reality check that things don't always work out. And when you're in a vortex, sometimes things suck.

The Space Cadet

Alex sat straddling the top of the LP gas tank, a large cylinder with two rounded ends, looking like some huge silver cold capsule sitting on its side in his back yard. On other days, this tank might have been an elephant he rode on safari, or a submarine he was rigging to explode. But today it was an interstellar space cruiser, and he pretended to work away at the rounded metal cap on the top, which today stood in as the antenna array.

"I've almost got it, Captain!" he called in a mock radio voice.

"No, you don't!" said his friend Mark, standing ten feet away and holding a red plastic squirt gun, which today stood in for his ray gun. "You'll never send that message! You'll never get help from the space station. You're dead!"

Alex jumped down from the tank and started running.

"Hey, it's zero gravity!" Mark protested.

"Oh, yeah," Alex said, and instantly shifted into a slowed-down pantomime of running.

Mark aimed his weapon and shouted, "Bzzzz! Got ya!"

"NO!" Alex cried. He recoiled from the pretend death ray and began to fall, still in slow pantomime. But before he hit the ground, he spun slowly around and with another "Bzzzz!" returned fire with his green squirt gun.

They both mimed a slow spin and a tumble to the ground just as the window opened and Alex's mother yelled, "Alex! Time for supper!"

Alex, instantly recovering from the effects of the death blast and zero gravity, stood up and said, "Mom, can Mark stay for supper and watch *Captain Video* afterwards with me?"

He looked over at Mark who, now similarly recovered, nodded with a smile.

"OK," Mom replied. "Come in and wash up."

"Son, what's your hurry?" Dad said at the supper table. "You're practically wolfing down your meat loaf and mashed potatoes."

Alex looked up and exclaimed, "It's almost time!" and then glanced hopefully at Mom.

"OK, since you have a guest, you can get out of clean-up duty tonight," she smiled. "Go on."

The boys scampered into the living room to warm up the Zenith in time to turn the channel knob to the Dumont network and hear the crackly voice of the announcer intone, "As he rockets from planet to planet, let us follow the champion of justice, truth and freedom throughout the universe. Stand by for…CAPTAIN VIDEO…and his Video Rangers!"

They stared at the grainy black-and-white graphic of static lettering superimposed over a background that looked vaguely like a nebula. They sat absorbed at the images, mostly long shots, of uniformed men mouthing urgent dialogue and wielding devices like an Opticon Scillometer (which looked suspiciously like an assembly of painted plumbing and wires). They watched rapt as one of the characters in the rear seat of a shuttle leveled his "cathode gun" behind the head of the pilot, who simply closed his eyes and fell forward.

Mark broke the silence by saying, "That ray gun is fake! No blast or nothing!"

Alex, oblivious to the slur, said, "That's what I want to do some day."

"What, make space shows with better effects?"

"No, be a space man. Really fly in outer space."

"Come on, you'll never be able to do that in your life."

"Why not? Grandpa says he grew up without airplanes, and now we have jets. He lived to see that. Who says we won't be traveling in space by the time we grow up?"

"Well, yeah, it would be cool. Just don't get swallowed up by some alien."

He was sitting on a mat or bed in some kind of chamber.   Its walls were smooth and clean. Metallic.   Titanium-colored.   The chamber was small and spare.   He saw no furnishings, no personal items.

He heard a constant thrumming sound emanating from some distance away.
The air was clean and sweet, rich and invigorating, but not fresh, not natural.   Obviously processed...how did he know that?

On the wall above him was a small round window, rather like a porthole. He stood up to look out.   He hadn't remembered looking through it before. From the window.... he could see the stars! He was in outer space!

"I had the dream again last night, Dad."

"Which dream?"

"The dream where I think I'm aboard a space ship. A real one. Out in space. And I was grown up."

"What were you doing there?"

"Well, I don't know. Nothing really. Just kinda looking around. I wasn't captain or anything. I didn't even see anybody else aboard."

"What do you think it means?" Dad asked.

Mom said, "It's probably nothing, dear."

"I know what my dreams mean," Alex smiled. "They mean I'm going to be a space man! An astronaut! I'll really be in space some day!"

"Son, they're just dreams," Dad said. "They can't tell us the future."

"Oh, no," Alex protested. "It's what I wanna be. I'm gonna study astronomy and physics and all that. I'm gonna do it!"

"Well, son, if that's what you want to do, go ahead and do it."

On his way upstairs after supper, he heard Mom say, "Are you sure you should encourage him like that? We really don't want to fill his head with notions."

"We could do worse," he heard his Dad say. "Look at Billy down the street. All he has on the brain is cowboys. He thinks he can be a cowboy and fight outlaws when he grows up. At least this'll get Alex to do well in science and math."

"But he's only nine. We shouldn't be feeding his fantasies."

"When I was nine I wanted to be a baseball star."

She chuckled. "Well, you didn't exactly turn out to be one."

"No, but it didn't hurt to wish for that, did it? Let's just let the kid have some fun. He'll grow up soon enough."

He was walking down a very large corridor. Its walls were mostly that same titanium color, with a slightly metallic sheen. Its lines were smooth, occasionally interrupted by lights and illuminated panels. He didn't think he had ever been here before. Off to one side was a door through which he could see a huge chamber filled with vegetation, including trees and plants with massive green leaves and multicolored flowers. Farther down he could just see into the window of one doorway. The room seemed to contain exercise or fitness equipment and a large pool, whose surface was not broken by a single ripple.

Of course interplanetary cruisers would be huge, he thought. And they would have amenities. People need living space. They can't just sit buckled into swivel chairs staring at control panels all the time.

But...where were the people? So far he had not seen anyone, nor heard any voices.

How big is this ship? he wondered. He really wanted to see into the bridge. But he apparently woke up before he could.

"Can I come down now?"

"Just a minute...OK!"

He slowly walked down the wooden steps into the basement. His dad had told him that he was working on a little surprise project, and that it would be ready this afternoon, but he couldn't come down to the basement workshop until it was finished.

His eyes popped open when he saw what lay in a corner of the basement. "Wow! This is great!"

Dad had cut a large oval out of plywood and set it up on a table in his play area. He had painted it a silvery blue and on it he had mounted rows of round plastic knobs, toggle switches, and assorted dials. He had even rigged a few red and white lights to an electric switch. On the right side his dad's gray metal World War Two tank radio microphone had been affixed to a bracket, its cord snaking behind the panel. In the top center, he had put an 8 x10 pane of glass in a frame, behind which he could slip various photos of planets and stars, simulating a view screen.

He had the bridge of a rocket ship in his basement!

He remembered the day they had been at the Jim's Radio Repair Shop, and his gaze had fallen on bins of used parts stacked along one wall. Where everyone else saw only dusty old knobs and tubes and switches, he saw rocket controls like the kind Captain Video and Rocky Jones and his crew were always turning and flipping on TV. "Aw…" he had let out. "These would make a neat control panel!"

His dad, the neatest dad in the universe, had said nothing at the time, but had remembered.

He barely took an instant to blurt out "Thanks!" before sitting in his command chair, picking up the mike, and announcing, "Rocky Jones, Commanding the *Galaxy*, requesting clearance for takeoff."

He played with it for nearly an hour that first day, imagining space battles and interplanetary races and distress calls and lots of takeoff and landing maneuvers.

For weeks afterward, he manned that control panel again and again, mentally transforming the entire house into a star ship.

A light began to flash in the wall opposite his bed. Several slots had been built into the wall; it occurred to him that he never knew what they were for. He walked over to them and noticed some half dozen illuminated buttons lined up above the slots. The flashing light was directly above them.

He pushed the first button on the right, and from the slot to the right emerged a small tray with silverware, napkins, ketchup, mustard, sugar, salt, and pepper. He pushed the second button, and out from the wall slid a silvery tray with a series of compartments, each containing a layer of paste-like substance of a different color. The largest one contained some brown stuff that smelled like beef stew. He tasted it. It tasted like beef stew. Surprisingly good beef stew.

He pulled up the chair and tried the substance in each tray in turn. The yellow stuff tasted like corn. Fresh corn, he thought. The yellowish white compartment yielded mashed potatoes. There was even chocolate pudding.

His hunger overcame him, and he cleaned off the tray. He felt, curiously, comfortable. He forgot for a moment the questions he had, the confusion he felt: Where was everybody? He had seen no one. He had heard no one. Who provided this meal? HE never ordered it. How did they know? And the larger questions that he now vaguely recalled thinking about before—how did he get here, and why?

And then he heard the voice—a loud, strong, deep voice. It did not seem to come from any speaker in the chamber. It seemed to resonate through his very being.

"I am Ming the Merciless! You have tried to free my slaves and destroy my planet, but it is you who will be destroyed! Prepare the death chamber!"

Over to one side, Alex, bound with a few wrappings of clothesline, replied, "You'll never get away with it, Ming!"

"Who shall stop me?"

Alex liked it when Mark played with him, because Mark was always willing to be Ming, which meant that Alex could be Flash Gordon. Mark threw himself into the role of villain. He borrowed a long cloak that belonged to his mother and draped it over him like a cape, playing Ming with stentorian tones and a great flourish of hands.

Three boys suddenly emerged from behind nearby trees, and as they ran up, one of them shouted, "We will! The Space Patrol has arrived!" His friends indifferently mixed up Flash Gordon and Rocky Jones and Captain Video and the Space Patrol, but Alex didn't care, because they could have more massive fights when they joined.

"Seize them!" Ming called to invisible guards. They always imagined a host of opposing guards or soldiers, so that each boy could claim victory over four or five of them. Flash broke free from his bonds, and they all launched into a pantomime free-for-all of punching and kicking and tumbling, complete with a chorus of mouthed sound effects for punches and ray gun blasts. The evil hordes were defeated, Ming the Merciless was vanquished, and peace and order were restored to the universe.

Then they all broke for lunch. Flash went home for a grilled cheese sandwich and tomato soup. He pointed out to his mom that in space, food comes in paste form in trays or tubes, but it still tasted good.

They played all summer. The hill over in the next block full of scrub grass and rock outcroppings stood in for an alien landscape, the monkey bars at the schoolyard became Rocky Jones' ship, and the farm equipment out in the yard at the implement dealership variously served as ships and space stations and wrecked hulks of downed space cruisers.

When school started in the fall, he could be counted on to select science fiction adventures for all his free reading, and his projects were always space- or astronomy-related. At those odd moments when the teacher's eye was less than watchful, he sketched ray guns and long, slender needle-nosed ships, always smooth and cylindrical with pointed fins at the end, and always belching flame and smoke from their sterns.

"You really like rockets, don't you, Alex?" Mrs. Johnson asked one day when she saw him drawing when he was supposed to be working on arithmetic.

"Oh, yeah," Alex said. "I'm going to go into space someday!"

"You are?" asked Mrs. Johnson. "Are you sure?"

"You bet!" Alex replied. "I know. I dreamed it!"

For Christmas he got a Space Explorer set with two helmets and two Atomic Ray Blaster pistols. It was terrific. The helmets had built-in walkie-talkies and the blasters made a zapping noise and shot sparks.

He and Mark played that afternoon. The accumulation of December snow in the yard meant that they could be on a frozen planet battling ice monsters. The process of getting into their parkas and snow pants and galoshes became the pre-mission ritual of donning their space suits in the decompression chamber. They could holster the blasters neatly into their coat pockets. As they put their helmets over their heads, Mom yelled, "Don't forget your stocking cap and earmuffs!"

Mom didn't understand. You don't wear stocking caps in a space helmet. And the earmuffs would just interfere with communications.

He felt something like a helmet being removed from his head. As it became detached, he felt sharp pricks in several spots around his head.

He did not remember what had happened while this helmet had been on; he now looked around the room as if he were seeing it for the first time. He was seated in some sort of metal chair, its metallic surfaces the same titanium color, its seat and arm sections cushioned in a soft brown leather-like covering. Intense blue-white lights glared down upon him. He could see very little beyond the glare. Some colored glass panels, some dials and screens, some cables. He heard the same dull thrumming sound he vaguely remembered.

He saw the entity lean forward and look down upon him with its large, empty, saucer-like eyes.

And he heard that voice. The same voice he had heard—or imagined—earlier. Nothing in the entity's face, if it could be said to have a face, moved, but the words came out: "We have completed our scans of your mental capabilities." Alex stared at him, wide-eyed. What did he mean?

"We shall now begin the probe into the physical nature of your being."

The what?

He felt himself lifted up, as if by some invisible force, and moved across the room and laid onto some kind of bed or cushioned table. In an instant, his head was clamped between padded restraints on either side. His limbs were held tightly by some force, perhaps some energy field, that he had never felt before and could not fathom.

He felt his entire body glide forward as if he were being slid into a large MRI chamber, like a train into a tunnel. A sharp, bleating noise blasted over and over. At intervals, a buzzing tickled his brain with its intensity.

He didn't know how long it lasted, but when it was over, the entity leaned over him again. He strained to comprehend what was happening to him. He tried to say, "What are you doing? Where am I?"

The voice soaring through his brain said, "Your mental images and visualizations were very amusing. What you might call 'quaint.' Perhaps they will distract you now."

My what? My mental images?

The devices that held him down were solid and unmoving. The walls were hard and smooth to the touch. The air was cool. The equipment beyond his sight hummed. Alex's nerves were awash with one sensory detail after another, so vivid and sharply defined that he came to the shocking realization....His jaw slacked and his eyes widened as the full comprehension crept into his consciousness....

"My God...you mean...this is not a dream!? This is real!!? NO!!!"

The entity began, oblivious to his screams of pain and terror, which were lost in the vastness of space.

Afterword to "The Space Cadet"

This is my attempt at a Richard Matheson/ *Twilight Zone* -type story.

August 18, 2005: I was browsing through the cheap videos at a video store and I saw some of those '50's and '60's cheapie science-fiction adventures like *Assignment: Outer Space*. I was reminded how I used to be into those, and how cheesy they were compared to more recent stuff like *Star Wars*. But I had fun imagining these fantasy adventures as a kid. And I've often thought that I couldn't write any sci-fi adventures because *Star Wars* and *Star Trek* had been there and done it all.

Then on the way home an idea hit me—have the main character be a kid who is imagining and playing these adventures with rockets and ray guns, etc., very 50's, and being in a real spaceship when he grows up. We flash from his childhood play adventures to these serious scenes aboard a more realistic ship, which he says he keeps dreaming about. But the kicker is that he really is on a space ship, as an adult, and they are seeing his memories. He screams at the realization.

I played this stuff as a kid. I had an LP gas tank in the back yard which figured prominently in my make-believe. I watched *Captain Video* and *Rocky Jones*. I played Flash Gordon lots with my cousins. My dad actually did make me a control panel out of plywood and knobs and switches bought at the local radio store, though not as elaborate.

I wanted to name the kid some 50's-sounding name like Butch or Bud or Buzz. But I had a cousin Butch, Buzz was too closely connected to Buzz Aldrin, Biff was too closely connected to *Back to the Future*, and I just did a story on Buddy. So instead I picked Alex as an homage to Alex Raymond, creator of Flash Gordon.

The Corners of My Mind

That woman came in again last night. Through the window. This time she stole my comb. I had my nice blue comb sitting right here on the dressing table, and today it's gone. I know she took it. She doesn't think I see her come in and go out, but I do.

I tell the nurse Judy. She just says, *Oh, I'm sorry, Cora. Maybe we can get you another one.* I don't want them to get me another one! I want them to lock those windows so those people stop coming in!

And where's Clarence? It's been days since he came to visit. He just forgot me and dumped me here. If I didn't know better, I'd say he was out with some floozy.

Time for breakfast. They make me walk there. It's really hard for me to walk, but they make me do it. I have to grab onto that railing all the way down the hall to the dining room. I don't understand why they have to be so mean to me. They say I need exercise. By the looks of some of them, so do they. Why can't they let me have that wheelchair? And all that money that Clarence pays for me to be here.

They're playing that awful music in the hallway again. Just loud enough to be annoying. Why can't they play what people like? Last week they played Barbra Streisand. Now that was nice.

Mary comes to visit. It's about time.

How are you, Mom?

"Tired. I didn't get any sleep last night because those people were making noise in the attic. And that woman came in through the window and stole my purse."

Stole your purse?

"Yes. The nice brown one."

Mom, you said you didn't like that purse. You said it was too small. We got you a nice new black one, remember?

"What new black one?"

This one. In the drawer here. See?

"That's the one that woman left when she stole mine."

No, Mom.   You said you didn't like the brown one.   Bill and I took you shopping last month and bought you this one.   You picked it out.

"Who's Bill?"

My husband.   Remember?

"Well, where is he?"

He's working.

"What time is it?"

It's two o'clock in the afternoon.

"I can't have anything nice.   They steal it all."

Mom, sometimes you forget.   You forget where you put things.   We all do.   It's normal.   You have to do what I do—get in the habit of having a set place to put something like your purse, and put it there all the time.   Then you don't have to think about where you put it.

"What time is it?"

It's just after two, Mom.

"I can't tell the time on my watch.   When am I going to get my new glasses?   I can't see anything with these. I told them that. Everything's all blurry. I can't read."

Mom, we took you to the eye doctor two weeks ago.

"No, you didn't.   I haven't been to the eye doctor in a year. Not since Clarence took me."

Mom, we took you two weeks ago.   You got an exam.   We had to go back the next day to pick up the glasses and try them, but you didn't want to go. You refused to get in the car.

"No, I didn't."

You said you were too tired. You shouted at me that you didn't want to go anywhere.

I don't know where she gets these stories. I didn't do that. I need new glasses and they won't get them for me. She lies to me. They all lie to me. It's like that time last year when she stayed out late with that Anderson boy on that date, and she lied to me about where she was. Clarence would have given her a licking but good if I hadn't stopped him. I shoulda let him. She screamed that she hated me. She thinks I don't remember, but I do.

Jacob the attendant comes in.

Good morning, Mrs. Ross. How are we today?

"Tired. And cold. Why don't you turn up the heat in here?"

It's 70 degrees, Mrs. Ross. When do you think you'd you like your bath?

"I had my bath."

That was Tuesday.

"What's today?"

Thursday.

"Jacob, those people came in again last night."

They did?

"Yes. And they stole my comb. Now when are you going to lock those windows so they can't get in? I asked you over and over to do it but you never do."

Mrs. Ross, the windows are locked. Every night. We wanted to keep them open for some ventilation at night, but you insisted they be closed, remember?   That's why it's warm in here and smells stuffy.

"Well, they're still getting in!   There are people walking around here all night!"

Of course there are, Mrs. Ross.   Attendants and nurses are on duty all night.   They walk the halls doing their jobs.

"No, they're stealing things.   And why didn't you lock the attic?"

Mrs. Ross, there's no attic in this place. And nobody is getting in at night!   You're imagining these things as a result of your vascular dementia. You have to understand that.

"I am not imagining it!   This place is not safe!"

Jacob, may I see you out in the corridor?

Mary takes him out there, and I think she's giving him a piece of her mind.   I sure would, telling me that I'm imagining things I know perfectly well to be true.   And then the floor supervisor comes over, and the three of them talk. A lot of head shaking and finger wagging.   Hah! I'll bet he got what for.   They should fire him.   All he does is argue with people.

Such   a   nice   anniversary   party   last week…my brother came from Illinois, and all my cousins…I hadn't seen them in years…we had presents and cards and a band…I had such a nice corsage…Clarence wanted to dance all night…we don't get to go out very much, so it was really nice… they played "Crazy" and "The Anniversary

Waltz"…and the cake that Mary and Bill got us was so good…chocolate marble swirl…with red and yellow frosting flowers. .. she said she was going to freeze some to save for us…I have to ask her whatever happened to that…and where's that crystal angel that they gave us?...I had it on the shelf in the house…I bet they stole that, too… .

Last week the nurse Stephanie, the nice one, gave me a diary. She said I should write things down, while I could still remember and my eyes were still good enough. What does she mean, while I could still remember? So I said, "What should I write?"

Oh, anything. What you did. What you ate. Who came to visit. What you thought.

And then she keeps asking me whether I wrote anything. So I write some stuff down just to make her happy and stop pestering me.

I tell Mary about the diary.

Can I see it? She reads my entries. Mom, you mostly put down what you had for meals and what you watched on TV.

"Well, what's wrong with that?"

How about what you thought about? What you remembered? Even, who came to visit and what you talked about?

"All right. How about all the lies the attendants tell me?"

Well, I guess you could write anything that's on your mind.

Mary brought Cory today. What a nice, smiling, freckle-faced boy. "Come here and sit on Grandma's lap." He does. He always does. "You know, I remember when you were born. Your mother was so thrilled. You were so small and pink. You giggled and smiled all the time. You called me Nana, because you couldn't say Grandma. I always liked it so much when your mother would bring you over. We played games. You always liked playing Uno. And croquet on the lawn. Your Grandpa would always cut the lawn nice before you came so we could play croquet. Do you remember that?"

Sure, Grandma. It was fun.

"So what grade are you in now? Fourth?"

Fifth, Grandma.

"See? I was close."

He works hard in school, Mom. He's getting good grades.

"Well, good. Now, Cory, I know that your mother is telling you to work hard and study in school, and that's important, but you need to have fun, too. You need to live life. Good times make good memories. Treasure your memories, because they'll be all that you've got left. I have such nice memories. I remember going to the county fair with Grandpa and your mother when she was about your age. We went on the rides and had ice cream and cotton candy. We had such a good time. Do you remember that, dear?"

Yes, I do, Mom. It was nice.

"And that house we used to live in with the screen porch? It was so nice to sit out there in the summer, with a nice lemonade or iced tea."

It was nice, Mom. I miss that house.

"Look at these blue jeans. They're worn and they're too small. That woman stole my good pants and left these. They stole my purse, you know. It was missing for three weeks. And then I found it again. They told me I forgot where I put it. But I know I didn't forget. It was stolen! It was stolen by those people in the attic. They brought it back after they took all the money out. I told Clarence to fix that window but he never did. For years I told him to fix that window. They're crawling around the attic all the time."

Mom, there's no attic in this place.

"Of course there is! I can hear them up there. Don't tell me there's no attic. You tell your Dad to go up there and nail that attic door shut so they can't get up there. I told him to a hundred times, but he didn't do it. Maybe if you tell him, he will. He doesn't listen to me."

She's rolling her eyes again. She thinks she does it in a way that I can't tell she's doing it, but I see her.

Jacob the attendant is pretending to straighten up the room and empty the baskets, but he's just being a busybody. I thought they fired him last week.

Mrs. Ross, you have to take your meds that Stephanie brought.

"I took them.   They don't do any good anyway."

No, you didn't.   You dropped some.   See, on the floor there?   And we found some dropped on the floor the other day, too.

"I didn't see that. I can't always see them. I told you my glasses are no good. Why don't you let me get new glasses?"

Mrs. Ross, you have to take all of your pills, every day.   If you don't take all of them, you won't feel good.   Your symptoms will recur.   You'll be agitated.

"Don't pick those up off the floor and make me take them. Get Stephanie. All you do is argue with me."

You know, this sucks.   I do my job and tell you the truth and you get mad and I get disciplined for it.

"Where's Clarence? I want to see him. Call Clarence!"

Clarence is dead, Mrs. Ross. And you need to take your meds.

"What? No, he's not! Don't say that!"

He's been dead for five years, Mrs. Ross! We tell you that all the time!   You can't even remember what we told you yesterday!

"He's not dead! I can prove it. Let me have my diary. I wrote down in my diary the last time he came here—last week. It's all here! Look!"

I grab my diary from the table and start paging through it to find the passage. They look like empty pages. I look closer. They try to take the diary away from me.

"No! It's right here! Just let me find it—the day he came. Where is it?"

Blank page... breakfast... Mary's visit... blank pages... what did they do to it?

It's not there, Mrs. Ross. There's no entry because he never came.

"You took it! You stole my pages to make me think I'm crazy!"

Lady, there never were any pages. You never wrote about him coming because he never came! I told you, he's dead!

The supervisor comes in.

Jake, leave the room! You're finished!

Hah? You can't fire me for telling the truth! Get out of here!

Two or three more come in. They start grabbing my arms, but I won't let them. "Let me go! Ow! You're hurting me! Get away from me!"

It's all loud and confusing. Breaking glass. The table knocked over. My shin hurts. Somebody grabs me. They pinch my arm. Then I see the needle.

"Don't stick that in me! Get away from me! Help! Help, Mary! Help, Clarence! Take me away from here!"

The radio was playing "You Don't Bring Me Flowers."

It's so nice on the porch. A warm summer breeze. It's early June. Probably about four. Clarence brings me a nice glass of lemonade, tall and frosty. Then he sits down on the chair next to me. Mary is playing on the lawn with the neighbor girl.

I can smell the tuna casserole baking in the oven, but it won't be ready for a while yet. We have time to relax.

It's a good life.

Afterword to "The Corners of My Mind"

This story is based on our experiences with my wife's mother, who suffered from vascular dementia as an after-effect of heart surgery and strokes. Most of the things Cora had in this story are things she had—the memory loss, the delusions, the insistence that her misperceptions were correct. She believed that strangers were living in the attic and that they repeatedly came in and stole her things. So she hid things, and then of course she forgot where she hid them, adding credence to her delusion.

My wife and I had many conversations about her mother and the difficulties of coping with her affliction. During one of these, I began to wonder what it would be like from her point of view, inside her head. She must be convinced, as we all are, that her view of reality is correct. So how does she think, from day to day, I wondered. What is her reality?

It wasn't hard to come up with examples of what she thinks. I just put down what she said or might say. The blue jeans, the purse, the locked windows, and the glasses are all incidents from her life. I just fictionalized them. I imagined this story as an exercise in stream-of-consciousness. I just needed to put a form to it, have some story arc. But, of course, she does not change.

Memories are so fundamental to our definitions of ourselves, to our very beings. I wanted a title with an allusion to some quote about memory.   I remembered that my mother-in-law liked Barbra Streisand, and the song "Memories" jumped out.   The other operative song lyric about memories that kept intruding itself, and showed up in her ironic advice to her grandchildren, was Paul Simon's   double-meaning   "Preserve   your memories; they're all that's left you."

Warm Bodies

He never knew in his wildest dreams that this moment would come, and yet here she was. She lay next to him, the smooth whiteness of her soft skin beckoning. He ran his hand up the curve of her warm thigh, over the hip, across the soft midriff and up to the firm, rounded breasts.

She gazed longingly up at him, her blue eyes still limpid in the dim light. Then she pulled him to her, hungrily. Her tongue snaked into his mouth.

He deftly inserted his ramrod and thrust, slowly at first, then stronger and harder, again and again, until she let loose one moan after another as she climaxed again and again. It was all he could *do to contain himself moment by moment, until he erupted in a torrent of ecstasy—*

"George! Dinner's ready!"

"Coming!"

George Crandall saved the document on his zip drive, closed the program, and shut down his computer. He detached the zip drive from its port and hid it where he always hid it, tucked down into the bottom of a plastic tray full of paper clips, erasers, batteries, and assorted office detritus in his desk drawer.

He left his den office and in a leisurely gait descended the stairs to the kitchen, where he sat down to his supper of baked chicken, mashed potatoes, green beans, and applesauce.

His wife Shirley brushed back a strand of graying hair and picked up the bowl of potatoes, saying, "I put a little garlic in the mashed potatoes. I thought I'd spice things up a little. Like 'em?"

He smiled a little between bites. "Um, they're fine, dear. I like the plain ones, too."

"What were you working on up there?" she asked between bites.

"Oh, emails. Mostly junk. Sure takes a lot of time to go through that stuff."

"You have to do the bills tomorrow, before they become due," she said, and then added, "And speaking of tomorrow, are you going to do the lawn?

"Yes, dear."

"And will you be getting around to cleaning up the garage next week?"

"I told you I would."

"And are you going to call that guy about the garage door?"

"Yes, dear. I called him yesterday and left a message. If he doesn't get back to me by tomorrow, I'll call again."

Shirley munched silently for a few moments, finishing her plate, and then said, "I've got a little ice cream. Want some?"

"Sure."

While she was scooping out the ice cream, she said, "So when we visit Sarah and the kids, are we going to leave that Friday night or Saturday morning? We need to call them."

He answered, "I thought we said Friday night. We can grab something to eat on the way, and then be there for all day Saturday."

"OK. Just wanted to be sure."

After supper, Shirley tended to the dishes and straightened up the kitchen while George sat down in the living room to watch TV. He watched a *Simpsons* rerun, then together they watched a *Seinfeld* rerun and *CSI*, after which she said, "Well, I'm going to bed. G'night, dear."

"G'night," he answered. He stayed up to watch most of the evening news, and then went upstairs to the bathroom. After brushing his teeth, he took his evening pills, including a tablet of Gas-X, and positioned a plastic adhesive Breathe Right strip across the bridge of his nose. Padding quietly into the bedroom, he changed into his pajamas and slipped into bed. As usual, Shirley was on her left side, turned away from him, already asleep, a lump in a flannel nightgown.   In ten minutes, he was asleep.

The following evening, when he walked in from the garage expecting her to be in the kitchen, he instead found her standing in the living room.

"What's this?" she asked as soon as he entered. She held up a sheet of white paper, slightly crumpled, on which passages had been typed, holding it between two fingers as if it had mouse droppings on it.

"I dunno. What's it say?"

"I'll tell you what it says," she said, and then read:

"The touch of her lips upon his shaft was like silk as she moved sensuously up and down, gently at first, then more vigorously, until he winced with delight..."

"Where did you get that?"

"I found it in the garbage, just by chance. The question is, where did *you* get it?" she demanded, her eyes narrowing. "Did you download this from some site?"

"No," he replied sharply.

"Well, where did it come from?"

George flushed a little. His lip quavered a bit. His eyes darted around. He looked down at the floor, then over at the lamp, then looked up vaguely in her direction.   He opened his mouth, then hesitated, took a breath, and said, "I wrote it."

"You what?"

"I wrote it. It's mine. It's an early draft. I didn't like the wording."

"What do you mean, you wrote it? It's disgusting!"

"It's a portion of a story. There's more to it."

"Story? This isn't a story! It's just pornography!"

"No, it's not. It's money in the bank."

"What?"

"I don't just write that. I sell it."

"What do you mean? How?"

"Just a minute. I'll show you." He went upstairs to the closet in his office, dug out a copy of a paperback book, and brought it back down to show her. She looked at it. It was called *The Old College Flame*.

"This is written by somebody called Brad Jason."

"That's me," he said. "People who write this type of material don't use their own names."

"And it's from the Hottbodd Publishing Company?"

"Yes."

She looked it over, thumbing through the pages, scanning a few passages. She read, "'She descended ravenously upon him'" and looked up. "Ravenously?"

"Yeah. My publisher likes words like that."

"My husband, the pornographer," she sniffed.

"We call it sexually explicit fiction. Porn is pictures or videos of people having sex. This is fiction, with a plot. And characterization. It also has sexually explicit scenes."

Her brow furrowed. "So when did you do this? How did you get it published?"

"About six months ago. I'd been working on the story for a year or two. I found a couple of publishers, and sent in a few things I'd done, and they picked this one."

"A few things? There's more? Why didn't you tell me about all this?"

"Well, look at your reaction. I wanted to wait for the right moment."

"The right moment? You mean after it's published but before our friends disown us and the police come and get you?"

"There's nothing illegal about this. Why should you be upset about it? The revenue from this book bought you that necklace last Christmas. And it'll pay for the garage door. And probably the new washer we need."

She mulled that over for a moment, but only a moment, before handing him back the book and saying, "Here. I don't want to have anything to do with this thing. I need some time to digest all this."

Over the next few days, George tried to gauge Shirley's mood, but without much success. She was not visibly peeved, and her tone was not particularly petulant. She was, if anything, a bit distant and subdued. Their conversations were mostly matter-of-fact, about household business or an occasional news item. He didn't know whether to bring the subject of his book up again, maybe even ask her to read some more of his stuff, or just try to forget the whole thing and move on.

The following Thursday she came home from the monthly meeting of her book club animated and upbeat for the first time in a week.

"Guess what?" she said.

"What?"

"We were talking about what to read next. One of the girls said we should read something more contemporary instead of the classics we've been doing. Sheri said she had always wanted to read *Peyton Place* and the subject got around to what you call 'sexually explicit material.' And Eleanor said we should try something like that. She said you'd be surprised what's in some of it, beyond the sex. And then she mentioned a title that her sister had given her. And you know what it was?"

"No," said George, not knowing where she was going with this.

"Your book!"

"MY book?"

"Yes. I nearly dropped my drawers. Eleanor!"

"So what did you say? Did you tell them it was mine?"

"No. I wasn't sure how to react, so I just listened and went along. It was strange to hear these ladies talk about sex scenes. Kind of, I don't know, exhilarating."

"Really?"

"Yes, isn't that something? She's lending it to Judith, who's going to pass it on when she's done. They're almost like giggly school girls. So I was wondering…could you lend me your copy?" She smiled a bit nervously. "I think maybe I'd like to take a look at it some more."

He did. And she did. Over the next few nights she sat in her favorite chair in the living room reading his book. He hesitated to ask her what she thought, waiting for her to broach the subject. He did notice that occasionally she smiled a little, or even chuckled, and once she dabbed her brow with Kleenex. He also found that at those times he could go up to his den and work on a manuscript without her inquiring what he was doing for so long at the keyboard. Rather than suggesting he should be attending to some household task instead of "wasting time" on the computer, she asked, "Are you writing some more?" And he no longer worried about leaving his zip drives out on the desk.

A few nights later, after she declared, as usual, that she was going to bed before he did, she rose and went up the stairs. Then she did something she rarely did. She called down, "Dear, are you coming up to bed soon?"

He answered, "Yeah, I guess I will be," and after a few minutes he turned off the TV and headed up the stairs. As he brushed his teeth in the bathroom, he thought he smelled a match. And there was an odd light coming from the bedroom.

He walked in and noticed that Shirley had just finished lighting a series of candles on the dresser and side tables. The room was bathed in a soft, warm glow.   Shirley was wearing a silky smooth negligee, scarlet with black ruffled trim, a garment he had never seen it before.

She turned and smiled to him, "Come on in, dear," and slipped under the covers.

He got into bed with her.

She descended upon him, ravenously.

Afterword to "Warm Bodies."

Gotcha. Did you think it was going to be some social comment or something? It's my doggy shag story.

This was my shortest, most quickly-produced story until "Out of Time" (I hesitate to call it a "quickie"). I thought of most of the main outline for it sitting in my chair at home for half hour on a Wednesday in October. The next day I began writing it on yellow legal pad in Hawke's Pub on State Street in Madison over Capitol Octoberfest, while waiting for my wife to shop. I had a good deal of it drafted by November, and essentially finished it off in mid-December.

Who are the people who write pornography? The stereotype is some pasty-faced guy with slicked-back hair and pencil-thin mustache, pounding away while sipping cheap scotch in a dingy office, or something. But who really does write it? I don't know, but maybe it could be an ordinary Joe, who leads an ordinary life filled with mundane details. Are the guys who write this stuff married? Do they have day jobs? Do they show their work to their wives? And what do their wives think?

Writers wonder about stuff like that.

Bed, Breakfast, and Beyond

Physical concepts are free creations of the human mind, and are not, however it may seem, uniquely determined by the external world.

--Albert Einstein, *The Evolution of Physics*

The eye sees only what the mind is prepared to comprehend.

--Robertson Davies

Steve Collier was in a funk.

The weather was beautiful, all right—sixty-eight, with partly cloudy skies and soft breezes. And the drive was beautiful—a gently undulating rustic country highway, snaking past bucolic barns and wood and stone fences. The meadows and cornfields had grown crisp and sere with the first touch of autumn, and clusters of hardwood forests bordering the roadways were just beginning to display swatches of gold and russet and maroon.

But his wife Abby was frowning. Again.

She fiddled with the FM tuner for several minutes, sampling stations, and then switched it off. "Nothing on the radio," she grumbled. Though she didn't say it, he could hear her add, "Dammit."

"Stick in a CD," he suggested.

"I've listened to everything. I shoulda brought more."

They rode on in silence for some minutes. He tried to admire the rolling countryside and the crisp foliage. He hesitated to bring up any topic of conversation, hoping that this little cloud would pass.

She broke the silence with, "Well, I don't need to go back to that restaurant again."

"Oh? You didn't like it? My soup and sandwich were good."

"My salad had olives and carrots in it, and I don't like olives and carrots. I hate having to pick them out. And the dressing was too sour."

"Didn't you say your soup was OK?"

"It was all right, but it wasn't great. At least it was better than that breakfast at that inn this morning."

"You said you liked it."

"I told the lady I liked it, to be polite. The way she described it to us last night, it sounded like it was going to be something gourmet. But it was just an omelet. It was ordinary."

"Well, it was hot and good, and there was plenty of it. With fruit."

"Melon is the cheapest fruit to serve. And those measly few strawberries I had were a little off. And the bacon was limp."

"I dunno, dear, it just seems that you expect so much."

"Why not? Why shouldn't we expect places who advertise a certain level of service to actually provide it? I mean, they charge enough for it."

He hesitated to say any more, but the road was long and the silence tedious. So he pursued the point. "You said you wanted to do a bed-and-breakfast tour of the Northeast, but after three days, you don't seem to have found much of anything you liked."

"Yeah," she acknowledged. "They all look so nice on line, but they've been pretty disappointing."

"Well, if this place coming up for tonight doesn't please you, maybe we should seriously rethink the idea of doing this again."

"You mean not travel?"

"Well, at least not go the bed-and-breakfast route. Or the motel route. You're not a fan of Super 8, either, remember. Something about musty odors, as I recall."

"So what's left? Camping?"

"Right. That'll never be a disappointment."

"Just watch the road," she said neutrally. "We should be coming up on the turn soon."

They entered the small town, slowing down to cruise past the ubiquitous gas stations, the strip malls, the McDonald's and Taco Bell, and turned down a street of two-story brick facades housing banks, boutiques, and bars. They continued on to a neighborhood of frame houses and pre-war bungalows.

On the third street down from the main drag, Abby saw the sign. "There it is. Ames Bed and Breakfast." Steve pulled over to park, and they looked at the place from across the street. They saw a plain two-story house in need of a paint job, sitting on a lawn dotted with crabgrass and in need of mowing. A rather weatherworn sign hung in the front lawn: "Ames Bed and Breakfast. Quality lodging."

"Looks a little shabby," she said.

"For once, I agree with you, dear. I'm disappointed, too. Now I see why they didn't put any shots of the exterior on the web page."

He thought for a moment, and said, "You know, according to the guidebook, this town is full of bed-and-breakfasts. We have a little time before we have to check in. Why don't we just drive around and see whether there are any others more appealing?"

"Really? You want to keep looking?"

"What's the harm? It won't take long. Who knows what we'll find?"

They drove down the street a few more blocks and turned the corner when they came to a wide avenue lined with towering oaks and elms. On both sides of the avenue stood stately, impressive two- and three-story homes, many nineteenth-century or early twentieth, with picket fences and wide, inviting porches.

"This is a nicer neighborhood," Steve said.

They were nearing the end of the street when Abby said, "Honey, look at that."

"What?"

"See the little sign there?"

He pulled over to get a closer look at the lettering: "The Great Expectations Bed and Breakfast?" he read. "It's really called that?"

"It's right up ahead," she said. "Let's at least check it out."

They drove farther down to where the street merged into a wide cul-de-sac amid large, wooded lots. The spacious, manicured yards had disappeared and merged into thicker woods, as if they had come to the edge of town. No other cars were around.

"What happened? Are we lost?" Steve said.

Abby pointed. "No, there it is."

Steve slowed to see a large, ornately-lettered sign on the side of the road:

The Great Expectations Bed and Breakfast
Everything you want in a B & B
Comfort, charm, the elegance of antiques and
carved woodwork
Fabulous breakfasts
And even a cat!

"Should we have a look at it?"

"Well, we've come this far."

He pulled the car over in front of a spacious yard of impressively-pruned birch, elm and ash, with well-tended patches of multi-hued flowers spread over a rich carpet of lawn.

"Wow, it looks really nice!" Abby said.

They got out and stood in the street and looked up to behold an exquisitely-maintained two-story Queen Anne-style Victorian manor with a rounded tower and pointed conical roof. It was flawlessly painted in the understated elegance of muted ochre and sepia tones with white trim around the windows and carved decorative moldings along the gabled roof lines. The main floor featured tall, arched leaded glass windows. The house was girded by a huge, wraparound porch with white railings. Curved, handmade willow and wicker chairs invitingly lined the porch, and baskets of ivy and geraniums in full bloom hung from the eaves.

And—wonder of wonders—an ornate shingle saying "Vacancy" hung from the signpost.

"This is what I've been looking for!" Abby said. "Let's look inside! What harm would it do?"

They found themselves almost drawn to the building. They walked up the veranda steps and opened the carved wooden entrance door inset with leaded glass. Inside the spacious hallway, they feasted their eyes on oak paneling, carved moldings, a textured ceiling, and an impressive oak stairway with polished rails and ornately carved newel post. It was like an inn that they had always visualized finding, but more richly detailed, more tastefully grand and elegant than any that they had ever actually been in before.

A white-haired, apron-clad woman, straight out of a Norman Rockwell painting, emerged from another room and greeted them.

"Hello. I'm Mrs. Worthington. Welcome to Great Expectations."

"Your sign said you have vacancies. What's available?" Steve asked.

"Oh, I'm quite sure I have something to your liking. Would you care for the tower suite?"

Abby smiled. "One of the things I've always loved about the Queen Anne style is the tower. I always wanted to get into the tower, and I never could."

"Well, now it's available!" Mrs. Worthington said brightly.

They took it. Abby was positively giddy about staying there. Steve didn't want to say anything, but he did not remember the last time she had been giddy about anything.

As they walked back to their car to fetch their luggage, Abby said, "What about the other place? We have reservations there."

He looked at his watch. "It's four-thirty. We have until five to cancel. I'll text them that we have to cancel." He did.

Back inside, Mrs. Worthington handed them their key and said, "Now you can come and go as you please, but one thing I do ask is that you respect the privacy of all our other guests. We like to think of each of our rooms as our guests' home away from home, so to speak. I'm sure you wouldn't want anyone looking into or poking around in your home. You understand."

"Of course," said Steve.

"Breakfast is at 8:45. I hope that's convenient."

"What's for breakfast?" Abby asked.

The kindly old lady smiled. "Something that will please you, I'm quite sure."

After Mrs. Worthington left, and they were walking up the stairs to their room, Abby said, "She could have told us what's for breakfast. What if it's something we don't like?"

Steve almost sneered, "Wouldn't that be a switch?" but instead just replied, "Well, that's the gamble you take at a bed and breakfast, isn't it?"

They ascended the winding oak staircase, replete with insets and niches of polished oak framing stained glass windows, and walked down the immaculate carpeted hallway to the door of the tower suite.

The door, like all the others in the hallway, was heavy, solid, and ornately carved, with gleaming brass hardware. They let themselves in.

They both gasped at the room. The bedroom was spacious, with a cherry wood four-poster bed prominent on one side, piled with plush pillows and facing an impressive stone wood-burning fireplace. Beyond that, in the tower section, they saw a charming sitting area with a French provincial chair on either side of a table with a Tiffany lamp and presenting a breathtaking view of forest outside the tower windows. The adjoining room featured a gleaming whirlpool bath and Italian tile, accented with plush towels and scented potpourri. They marveled at the antiques, decorative candles, and other quaint touches that abounded throughout.

"Oh, my God, this is really beautiful!" Abby exclaimed.

"You like it?"

"Who wouldn't like this?" she replied.

Steve added, "And that's the quietest air conditioning I've ever heard."

Abby said, "I can still hear it. Oh, wait, not really." Steve smiled.

They began to unpack. As she was hanging some blouses in the closet, Abby stopped for a moment and looked at the side table next to the doorway. She said, "You know, this is a nice table, but remember that carved mahogany table with the oval marble top that we saw in the antique store last week? Boy, that would really go nice here."

"Yes, I guess it would."

"Yep, it would be just about perfect there."

Steve flopped on the queen-sized four-poster bed strewn with decorative pillows and said, "Hey, we can see the fireplace beautifully from here. Let's see if the TV works." He picked up the remote from the bedside table and surfed through several channels. "Nice reception," he commented, then added, "I have to turn a little to see it. I'll have to watch how I sit. Hate to get a crick in the neck."

Abby sat down in the parlor chair in front of the window in the tower portion. "Nice reading lamp," she said, admiring the Tiffany shade, and then added, "The chair's not too comfortable, though."

"You're doing it again," Steve said.

"What?"

"You said you liked the place. You said it was charming, and all that. So we took it. And now as soon as we're moved in, you start to pick away at it. This isn't quite right, and too bad that isn't different, and so on. It's as if the place has to be perfect. It can't ever be good enough."

"I'm not saying it has to be perfect. I'm just making a comment."

"No, you're nitpicking," he replied. "You're finding tiny flaws and making a point of them. You always do it. If you were looking at a beautiful hand-woven Oriental rug, you'd be too distracted by one piece of lint on it to see the beautiful pattern."

"Oh, don't be ridiculous," she said. "You're exaggerating."

"So where do you want to go for dinner?" he asked, changing the subject.

Nearly two hours later, they returned from dinner. As they climbed the stairs, Abby was finishing her cavil about the meal. "The steak was overdone," she had been explaining. "I order it medium rare and it almost never is. And the soup was too salty. Restaurant soup is always too salty."

"I guess mine was a little better than yours," Steve said as he inserted the key into the oak door. They entered the tower suite and switched on the lights. "How about a long, soothing bath?" he asked. He turned to empty his pockets and place his wallet and change on the table next to the doorway.

But instead of the decorative oak side table that he remembered, there sat an elegantly carved, mahogany side table with a smooth gray-white marble top.

"How did this marble-top table get here?" he asked.

"What?"

"This table. It wasn't here when we left."

"Yes, it was," she replied.

"No, a different table was here. An oak one, remember? You said you thought that table we saw in the antique store would be perfect here. And now here it is. The very same table."

"What I said was a marble-topped table would be just what I would expect here. And that's what's here."

Steve furrowed his brow a little. "Dear, you were very specific. You wished that a table that was *not* here, was here."

"You're not making sense. Why would I wish for a table that was already here, and just what I expected?"

Steve let it go. It wasn't worth arguing about.

"Look at this," she said, after bending down to open the carved hutch beneath the bookshelf. "A bottle of cabernet, here in the cabinet. And two Waterford crystal glasses."

"Cabernet's your favorite," he smiled. "I didn't know that was included in the room. Mrs. Worthington must have put it there while we were gone."

"Yeah. Funny she didn't tell us that was included, though."

He opened the wine and poured them each a glass. Steve savored a sip or two from his delicate stemmed glass, commenting, "This wine is terrific."

He reclined on the bed for a moment and then said, "Dear, you remember I said I had to turn my head a certain way to see the TV from the bed, and I thought I would get a crick in my neck?"

"Yes."

"Well, now I'm sitting here and I'm looking straight on at the TV, and it's quite comfortable."

"Well, good," she said, half listening while she rummaged through the suitcase.

"That's not what I mean. I mean that the TV cabinet used to be to the left of the bookshelf," he said. "The bookshelf used to be next to the fireplace. Now the TV cabinet is located between the bookshelf and the fireplace."

"What do you mean, 'used to be?'"

"I mean it moved since we left."

"Don't be ridiculous. It was always this way."

"Are you positive?" he asked.

"Well, I don't remember looking at it all that carefully, but how could it be otherwise?"

"Right. And how could a table that wasn't here suddenly be here?"

"I'm going to get a couple of the magazines from the cabinet downstairs," she said. "You want anything in particular?"

"No," he answered.

She left and returned a few moments later. As she turned the door knob to re-enter the room, she noticed that their neighbors down the hall had their door open for just a moment. She could see that it was dark and smoky inside, with what looked like a strobe light. Loud music and raucous, noisy laughter poured out of the room. A girl stepped out of the door and into the hallway, a girl dressed in a tight black skirt, with dyed spiked magenta hair, tattoos on both arms, and at least four piercings hanging from her face.

"Did you guys call for more ice?" she shouted to someone within. "Here it is, right here in the hallway!"

She glanced up to see Abby, and Steve behind her, looking at her. "Oh, sorry," she said, and she closed the door again.

"Wow," Abby said. "Must be a real party going on in there."

"That's funny, dear," Steve said after a moment. "Did you notice that?"

"Notice what? Her tattoos?"

"No." He cocked his head. "There's no noise. And I can't smell any smoke. It's just a quiet, empty hall way, just like before. You wouldn't even know there was a loud party going on. Boy, whatever they use to insulate this place, they should sell it to college dorms!"

She began to change into her lingerie when he added, "Speaking of a real party, let's have a little party of our own." She smiled at him.

He poured her some wine and they talked and laughed for a half hour. They found a cache of

DVD's in a compartment at the base of the bookshelf. They watched a romantic comedy that they had both heard about but had never gotten around to seeing. They smiled in amusement throughout. When they drained the first bottle of wine, they found, to their surprise, another bottle in the cabinet, and they opened and savored that one as well.

They craved some music. The room was furnished with a nice CD player and a collection of CD's. Steve browsed through them, expecting to find the usual clichéd offerings of New Age harp and dulcimer or piano music. But to his surprise, he found a Modern Jazz Quartet album of soft, mellow jazz, which they played while they made passionate love. Abby had to admit it was all better than she thought it could be.

They awoke at 8:20 a.m., entirely rested and refreshed. They realized that, having lost track of time the night before, they had neglected to set an alarm. Yet they now seemed to have just the right amount of time to dress and get ready. They appeared in the doorway of the downstairs dining room at precisely 8:45.

Mrs. Worthington, clad in a bright pink apron, breezed in through swinging wooden doors on the other side of the room. "Good morning!" she chirped with the brightest morning smile they could imagine. "Your beverages and bakery and fruit are set. I'll be out with the entrees in a jiffy. Enjoy!" She glided back into the kitchen.

They sat down, on handsome leather-backed chairs, to a table set with linen and lace, with a china pattern and crystal that Abby thought was impressively elegant. Before them in tall crystal sat fruit parfaits, artfully layered pieces of perfectly ripe fruit and lemon-zested crème fraiche. They sampled the chilled juice blend from the Depression-glass goblets. "A really interesting blend," Steve said. "I can't identify all the different juices, but it's really delicious."

The steaming coffee, already poured into their cups, was rich French roast, Abby's favorite. A basket of at least four different kinds of hot, fresh rolls tempted them with intoxicating aromas. They indulged in all of them, finding each flakier and more savory than the last.

In a few moments, Mrs. Worthington waltzed in, bearing a mounded breakfast platter in each hand. In front of Steve she placed a platter laden with thick slices of brioche French toast, grilled golden brown, covered with a mound of berries and pastry crème, all sprinkled with powdered sugar. Accompanying the French toast were two sausage patties, perfectly grilled, lean and savory.

Before Abby she laid a platter bearing the thickest, fluffiest Belgian waffle Abby had ever seen, also mounded with fruit and sprinkled with powdered sugar. Accompanying the waffle was a plate with rashers of perfectly crisp, coppery bacon strips.

Abby took a bite of the waffle. "Oh, my God, this is a heavenly. And this bacon is just the way I like it." She savored the bite and then asked, "How is it that you gave us different items? I've never heard of that in a B and B."

"Are they not to your liking?" asked Mrs. Worthington.

"Oh, no, quite the opposite. It's fantastic. But how did you know that he likes French toast and I prefer waffles?"

"Oh, I just had a sense about what you would like. Call it intuition," she said with a twinkle in her eye.

For dessert, Mrs. Worthington served them each a stemmed dish of Depression glass bearing scoops of lemon, lime, and raspberry sorbets bathed in champagne, with a sprig of fragrant lemon thyme delicately speared on the top.

Abby noticed that Mrs. Worthington disappeared into the kitchen for most of the meal, reappearing only at just the right moments to whisk away dishes. So many B and B hostesses, she had observed, hovered around their guests as if they were waiting for compliments, sometimes even sitting down with them and chatting endlessly. Abby always found that tiresome.

When they returned to their room, Abby, having decided to do a little reading, sat down on one of the chairs in the tower sitting area.

"That's odd," she said.

"What?"

"This chair. It's so comfortable. And isn't this a different upholstery than it had before? It's softer."

"What do you mean? Isn't it the same chair?"

"That's what I'm getting at," she said. "I don't know. It doesn't seem the same."

"I guess it does seem different," he allowed. "But she wouldn't have changed the furniture in that time, would she?"

To their surprise, they rarely saw or heard any other people in the house. After lunch, Abby talked Steve into roaming the rather labyrinthine halls of the second floor, and then the first. Her curiosity provoked, she wondered about what sorts of rooms might be behind all the closed doors she found. She did happen to run into a couple in the main floor lounge, and they struck up a conversation with them. They introduced themselves as Chad and Laura, and they said they loved the place and had visited often.

"We've stayed in many B and B's, and this is really the finest. Head and shoulders above the rest," Laura said. "What's your room look like?"

"Oh, it's just beautiful," Abby chirped, "with carved oak woodwork and a big four-poster bed and a gorgeous view. Even a working fireplace, with wrought-iron andirons."

Laura waved her hand dismissively and said, "Oh, that sounds like so many places we've been to. We used to go for that look, too. But carved woodwork and antiques are so passé. We've gotten tired of the same old thing, all the oak and Depression glass, and we came here because we wanted something different."

Steve furrowed his brow. "Different?" he wondered. "If you were looking for something different, why go to another antique-filled Queen Anne home?"

"Oh, this is hardly an antique-filled Queen Anne home," she said.

"It isn't?" Abby asked, puzzled.

"Would you like to see our suite?" said Chad.

Steve hesitated. "We would, but, well, Mrs. Worthington was quite particular about not going into anybody else's room."

"Oh, that's without permission. We're inviting you! Come on!"

Abby and Steve were taken aback to see that the décor of Chad and Laura's room was a stylish Swedish modern. They saw solid dark blue walls, sleek blond oak tables and chairs, a curved leather sofa with black pillows, and a sleek faux-glazed marble electric fireplace with holographic flames in muted pastel colors. Subdued New Age music circulated in the background.

They looked upward to see that the ceiling rose to accommodate a second-story loft lounge, with a big-screen TV and stacked black stereo components. The lounge was furnished with stylish, very contemporary-looking reading chairs.

Japanese and expressionist art prints hung on the walls.

"My God," Abby said. "This is something else. I didn't realize they even offered a room like this."

Steve added, "Yeah. This doesn't really seem consistent with the look of the place or its image in the ads."

"Well, the ad we saw mentioned it. When we described what we were looking for to Mrs. Worthington, she said she had just the thing. We love it. We'd like to decorate our house this way!"

He opened a sleek ebony wall cabinet and reached in for a bottle. "Care for a little Absolut Citron?"

Back in their suite, Steve and Abby sat on the bed, silent for a moment .

"Do you think that bottle of Absolut came with the room?" Steve asked.

"Why? Did you want one? We got a bottle of wine, remember? Two, actually."

"That vodka's pretty expensive to be complimentary."

"But you don't like vodka," she countered. "And you loved the wine. I don't think the wine was cheap, either."

Abby thought for a moment, and then added, "I still don't get it. Why would they come to an inn that looks like this if that's the kind of room they wanted? Why would an inn like this even *have* a room like that?"

Steve stood at the tower windows and stared out, momentarily distracted by the view of the impressively-manicured yard and dazzling fall colors on the birch and elm trees. Then after a moment, he said, "It doesn't add up."

"What doesn't?"

"The changes in furniture in here, the décor in the other rooms, Mrs. Worthington's incredible intuition…."

"Quit trying to figure it out," Abby said. "You're doing what you always complain about me doing—making something out of nothing."

Steve ignored her comment and continued, "It's like Chad and Laura didn't see what we saw in the building. I can't really explain it, but I have a very weird idea."

"What?"

"Come with me," he said. "I want to check something out."

He led her outside, where they stood on the lawn in front of the inn, far enough away to take in the entire building in their view.

"Abby, look at the house," Steve said. "What do you see?"

"What do you mean? It's a beautiful, two-story painted lady with four gables and a rounded tower. Same as it was when we arrived. So what?"

"Where do you think *their* room is?"

"Huh?"

"We were just in a two-story room on the second floor, a room with at least a fifteen-foot ceiling. Where in this house right in front of you could that room possibly be?"

"I can't tell. Maybe in the back part," Abby surmised, and then added, "It doesn't seem to be a big enough house to contain that kind of room."

"Exactly."

"What are you getting at?"

"I don't know. It just doesn't make sense. But I think we should leave."

"Leave? Why?" she asked.

"Because this is just too weird. There's something about this house that's...I don't know...."

"You see a few things you can't readily explain, and you want to leave?"

"It's more than just a few things," Steve replied. "They are things that defy explanation, common sense, the laws of physics."

She hummed the *Twilight Zone* theme.

He snickered. "OK, fine, be sarcastic. But you can't explain it, either."

"I don't want to explain it. I just want to enjoy it. You said you liked the place. Now who's finding faults?"

"I do like the place. I did, anyway."

"Well, why don't we just stay a little longer, and maybe all this will sort itself out? We'll talk to Mrs. Worthington. After all, we've only been here one night."

He looked at her, his expression suddenly somber. "Abby, we've been here three nights."

"What?"

"We've been here three nights! It's Friday! You enjoyed it so much you wanted to extend our stay. You said it exceeded your expectations. Mrs.

Worthington was quite pleased and eager to accommodate, as I recall."

They walked back upstairs, Abby's thoughts a confused swirl as she tried to recall all of the events of the past few days. As they reached the door of their suite, she became anxious.

"I don't know that I want to go in."

"Why?" Steve asked. "It'll be exactly what you expect. You can be sure of that."

"I still don't get it," she said. "The room can change itself? You've got to be wrong about this. There's another explanation."

"Look, I have an idea," he said. "You're going to think it's crazy, but indulge me." He looked directly into her eyes. "We have to both create an expectation. Concentrate on wanting something. Something that can go in the room."

"Like what?"

"How about that cuckoo clock that we saw in the antique store? You remember, the one with the little boy and girl and the wood cutter—the one with the delicate carvings? You spent a long time looking at it."

"Yes, I remember."

"Think about it. Think hard about it. Visualize it, in detail. Wish that it was in the room."

"Wish for a clock in the room?"

"Not wish, exactly. Expect it. Imagine it fitting into the room. Imagine it was always there, because it belongs. Try hard."

They both stood there and concentrated on mental images of the clock. They tried hard to think of nothing else. After a few moments, Steve felt the thought pass, almost as if it had been pushed out of his mind.

Abby sighed and looked up. "Well, I tried. Did you?"

"Yes." He looked into her eyes again, and then they both cocked their heads. They heard a lilting cuckoo. He opened the door to their room, and there it was—a beautiful carved Swiss cuckoo clock mounted on the wall, the miniature Swiss-garbed boy and girl twirling, the little gray cuckoo popping in and out sounding the hour.

Abby screamed, her shriek melding with the dying trills of the cuckoo.

Steve held her as her gasps ebbed and said, "Convinced?"

"Steve, what's going on!?"

"There's only one explanation," he replied grimly. "The house is changing. Morphing itself to conform to the expectations of the guests."

"What!?"

"I know it sounds crazy, but—"

"You're the one who sounds crazy!"

He grasped her shoulders. "All I know is we have to get out."

She pulled back from his grip and snapped, "Just when I find some place I really like, you want to go!"

Befuddled, he shook his head in disbelief. "We have to leave."

"No!" she exclaimed.

"Abby, we have a life out there. We have to get back."

"Why? I like it here!"

Steve shivered at the glazed expression in his wife's eyes. She was becoming distraught. He pulled his wallet out to withdraw a photograph and showed it to her. "Abby, this is our daughter, Marissa. She's coming to visit us from Seattle next month. Look! Remember her?"

Abby looked at the photo a moment and then said, "Can't we just invite her here? I'll bet Mrs. Worthington will let us reserve a room for her. Wouldn't that be fun? We can make this room any way we want! We just proved that."

"Abby! You have to snap out of it! Look!" He pulled out another photo. "Here's a photo of you standing in front of our house."

She stared at the photo for a moment. "But this looks so… so ordinary."

He grasped both her arms again and implored, "We have to go back. We have to leave. Think about that, Abby!"

She gazed back and forth alternately between the photos of Marissa and the house. After a moment, she hesitated, and then shuddered. A tear came to her eye. "So what I have to do," she murmured, "is expect to go home?"

"That's right," Steve said, putting his arm on her shoulder. "Vacation's over, dear. No other expectations. Just home."

At the bottom of the stairs stood Mrs. Worthington, her brow furrowed, her demeanor more somber than they had seen before.

"You figured it out, didn't you?" she said in a voice lower and coarser than they remembered.

"Yes."

"Ah, that's a pity. Most folks leave here never knowing the truth. Or caring."

"So, what, we're just more perceptive?" asked Steve.

"That's one word for it. Picky would be another. Sometimes we're just too skeptical for our own good. Tell me, what did it? Was it the clock?"

"Well, that was pretty incredible."

"I couldn't help it. Once the die is cast, I can't entirely control it."

Steve said, "I just have to ask…how? How does it happen?"

"Oh, I can't tell you that. There are things in life that just can't be explained. Let's just say I have a gift, a talent."

Abby said, "Well, then how about why?"

Mrs. Worthington smiled. "Why not? Why not make people happy? Artists and writers and musicians use their talents to make people happy. Life is full of frustrations and disappointments. Shouldn't everyone be entitled to a little unalloyed pleasure once in a while, to have something exactly as they want it?"

"An ability like yours could eliminate discontent and envy," Steve said. "It could change the world—"

"No, it couldn't," she cut him off. "All I can handle is my little corner here. That's all I care to handle."

"But this is phenomenal," Steve pressed, gesturing broadly. "The world should know about this!"

Mrs. Worthington wagged her finger and pursed her lips. "If you have any ideas about bringing any portion of world attention here...," she trailed off, "well, you won't find me if you try. No, some things are best in small doses. Just let it go. Go back to your life and content yourself with the fact that you had a nearly perfect getaway to treasure. Isn't that worth something?"

Steve frowned and shook his head a bit. "But that's it? We just leave? We're just free to go?"

"What, did you think the house was going to kidnap you or something? This isn't a Stephen King story." She smiled devilishly and added, "Though, if that's what you expected, it could be arranged. But no, you're free to go."

They found their luggage packed and sitting in the hallway outside the carved oak door of the room. Abby could not resist opening the door to take one last look at the room.

She was taken aback. The room was empty. A plain, nondescript carpet lay on the floor. The walls were dingy drywall and the bed was nothing more than a frame with a box spring and mattress, with no bedclothes. It smelled a little musty.

As they walked out to their car with their luggage, they met a young woman carrying a valise and handbags on her way up the walk to the house. Her brown hair was drawn back in a bun. She wore wire-rimmed glasses and a shaggy cardigan over a floppy sun dress. She stopped a few feet in front of them, looked up at the house to their backs, and gasped, "Oh, my God, it's beautiful!" Then she turned to them and asked, "Are you just leaving? Did you stay here?"

"Yes," Abby answered.

"How did you like it?"

Abby looked at her husband and said, "Truthfully, I'd have to say we loved it and we're sad to leave."

She set down her valise and cloth carrying tote with the wooden grips, adjusted her glasses as she looked up at the inn, and said, "I heard about this place from some friends. They just raved about it. It looks like just what I'm looking for! I brought a bagful of books, and I plan to just curl up in front of a crackling fire and forget about my job and my troubles for an entire weekend!"

"Well, have a good time and enjoy yourself," Steve said, and they moved on.

As she passed them, they turned to watch her continue up the walk. To them, the building she approached looked like a warehouse, a squarish cinder-block building with a corrugated metal roof and sitting on a dirt yard with spotty patches of yellowed grass.

Abby furrowed her brow. "So is this what she expected to find?"

"No, this is what the place really looks like," Steve replied. "We are seeing it as it is. Because that's what we now expect. The place does not want to attract us. We don't meet its expectations. It wants her now."

"Well, shouldn't we tell her?"

"What, and spoil her nice weekend?"

Afterword to "Bed, Breakfast, and Beyond"

I dreamed this story. I really did. I've almost never dreamed a complete story before, with a beginning and a complicating arc, all the way to a solution. But this one came to me out of whole cloth, and even more amazing, I remembered it after waking.

My wife had given me a copy of Stephen King's *Nightmares and Dreamscapes*, and I had read two of the stories in it beforehand. They were both about a couple stumbling onto a place which on the surface seems nice, but then getting ensnared by the weird supernatural power and influence it wields. That had to be where it came from, I guess.

When I told Amy about it, she said, "Well, are you going to write it?" I didn't know whether I wanted to. I didn't know whether the idea was any good.

And then as it rumbled around in my mind, I realized that it could be a story about complaints, expectations, and disappointments, which are universal. So I thought maybe it could be fun.

The story is somewhat in the Stephen King style, though nobody dies and nobody is menaced with bodily harm (though maybe that's just because they get out in time…?).

Jerry

Two o'clock. They would start arriving any time now. Michael Fitzpatrick had a lot to do before they got here.

In his nearly six weeks on the job at The Fairview Home, Michael had learned that at visiting time, everything had to be right. After lunch cleanup in the dining room, he had to vacuum the hallway leading to the common area, and then he and Hector had to do a final sweep through the common area—no litter, no dust, fire lit in the marble fireplace, everything arranged in its place.

Then it was time to escort the clients from their rooms out into the common area. Some could walk on their own, needing only a reminder of what time it was. Some needed to be held by the arm. Mr. Kowalski needed to be wheeled in. Mrs. Olson insisted that she could manage just fine with her walker, but Michael needed to hover next to her anyway. Mrs. Adams, as usual, was befuddled, wondering, "What? Where are we going?" Mrs. Gonzales went reluctantly, grumbling that nobody comes to visit her anyway and she just wanted to watch TV.

One by one they paraded out into the common area and took their places on the French provincial chairs and leather sofas or sat at the walnut tables.

The visitors began to arrive. Michael watched their faces. They ambled in with smiles and pleasantries in upbeat voices, taking their loved one's hands, looking expectantly into the often-vacant eyes, hoping that today they would be recognized, that today Grandma or Uncle Bert would remember a little more. They looked for that spark of recognition, that recollection of the past they once shared.

As the sunlight filtered in through the tall windows and the conversations wore on, Michael could tell when things began to wind down. Watches were glanced at, smiles became labored, young children got squirmy—he saw it all every week.

He saw how frustrated the relatives became after a while. Most visitors could only take so much of explaining one more time who this or that person was, or listening to the grousing about when their family was going to take them back home, usually to a home that had long ago been emptied and sold.

For many of the visitors, especially the ones who had been coming for years, the visits were more ordeal than pleasure. The longer the patients stayed here, the less often they got visits.

And then there was Mrs. Barnes.

She had been here the longest, Michael had been told—eight years. She was far and away the nicest client in the wing. Her room was always tidy. She dressed and groomed herself immaculately, meticulously picking out her clothing and jewelry, especially before visits, and always checked herself in the mirror before going out to the common areas.

Dr. Finley, the director, described her Alzheimer's as advanced, the worst on the floor. She had no idea who she was, Michael had soon learned. Sometimes she responded when they called her "Mrs. Barnes" or "Lucille." But other times not. She knew her way around the facility, and could always find her way back to her room, but that was about all.

Most of the other patients could remember key events in their lives, and their names and the names of at least their closest family members, even though they might sometimes be unclear as to whether the family members were alive or dead. But to Mrs. Barnes, Michael observed, every day seemed to be the only day of her life. She had no idea how long she had been here, or what her life had been like before she came. The old photos in her family albums were just interesting pictures of people she didn't know.

But that didn't discourage the man from coming to visit her. He was six feet tall, always dressed in a tailored suit, and his graying, well-barbered hair and distinguished middle-aged handsomeness presented quite the figure. When he entered the common room, he turned the heads of more than one visiting daughter or wife.

He came twice a week, sometimes three. He always greeted her the same way. "Hello, Mother. How are you today? I'm your son Alan."

Sometimes her response was a puzzled "Son? I don't have a son." Sometimes it was "My son is dead." Today it was just the generic "You are? I'm sorry, I don't remember."

He sat and chatted with her for at least a half hour, often longer. Michael could not help but notice that no matter what she said, no matter how certain she might be that he was not her son, his reaction was always kindly and understanding. He nodded, smiled pleasantly, and just went on conversing with her, completely ignoring that she denied knowing him. Christ could not have been more even-tempered to the thrice-denying Peter.

He asked simple questions, often the same questions every week, about her health, her meals, how she enjoyed the activities. If she hesitated or couldn't remember, he seemed to be not at all flustered or impatient at that, but simply moved on to the next question. Today was no exception.

It came to the point where he said, "Well, you look a little tired, Mother. It's been so nice seeing you, but I must be going."

"Oh, you do? Well, if you must. Thank you for coming to visit me." Michael could hear in her voice the unspoken "whoever you are." But Mr. Barnes simply smiled graciously and departed.

As they watched him leave, Michael said to Hector, "Look at that guy. He's a freakin' saint. He's never discouraged. Why does he keep coming?"

"Why do any of 'em keep coming?" Hector replied. "It's like that movie *The Notebook*. There's always the chance, you know that one of them will snap out of it and be themselves for a little while. It happens."

"But you told me she never recognizes him. There's never been a glimmer."

"Yeah, well, I guess it's hard to give up hope," Hector shrugged.

For some time, Michael had wanted to ask Mr. Barnes what the secret to his patience was. He wanted some insight into how family members coped. Mr. Barnes was obviously wealthy—he always arrived in a chauffeured limousine—but all his money couldn't buy his mother back for him.

The staff was discouraged from anything but brief social conversations with the relatives during visiting hours. But today Michael thought that a quick talk with Mr. Barnes on the way out would do no harm.

He followed Mr. Barnes out the main entrance and down the paved walkway. As Mr.

Barnes neared the parking lot where his limo waited, Michael called, "Mr. Barnes!" He saw the man stop and begin to turn around. But at that same instant, Michael was distracted by what he heard from the left. Manuel, in his golf cart loaded with his landscaping gear, came tearing across the yard. Manuel had been reprimanded before for tooling around on the grounds so fast, but again today he was rolling in too fast, the jerk.

"Look out!" Michael shouted.

Mr. Barnes saw Manuel approaching and stood there, in what Michael thought was an odd stance. He seemed to hesitate and awkwardly, mechanically, shift his weight from one foot to the other, as if he were uncertain how to react.

Manuel beeped his little horn, swerved around Mr. Barnes, and sped off without even looking back.

Mr. Barnes spun half around. Michael knew he had not been hit, but he seemed to pitch unsteadily on his feet. Then he tottered and fell down onto a cluster of landscaping rocks beside the walk. Michael could tell that he hit his head.

He rushed over to help. He looked down at Mr. Barnes lying on the ground—and gasped.

His head had been torn nearly off.

But that was not what made Michael gasp.

Snaking out from the large V-shaped gash in Mr. Barnes' neck were wires and pieces of circuitry. Sparks sputtered, and some oily liquid oozed out. The strangely blank eyes stared upward, the mouth opening and closing. Flesh had been scraped from the right cheekbones, revealing more wiring and sputtering circuitry beneath. Mr. Barnes' right arm lay limply askew on the lawn as if it had been broken, but it twitched mechanically. A faint whiff of acrid smoke rose from the body.

Aghast, Michael stared down at the sight, in shock.

In an instant, two black-suited men leaped out of the limousine and rushed toward Mr. Barnes. Quickly, efficiently, they picked up the mechanism, the thing that was Mr. Barnes, and carried it hastily to the limo, where they deposited it in the back seat.

One of the men turned to Michael and said gruffly, "You didn't see anything."

"I didn't see anything!?"   Michael exclaimed, shocked.

The man pointed emphatically and said, "Just forget about it." They climbed into the limo and roared off.

Michael did not know what to do about what he had just seen. Part of his brain was convinced that such a thing could not even be. But he had seen it. It was no illusion.

His mind was a whirl as he thought about what to do. He looked around and noticed that, evidently, no one else had beheld what he had. Manuel probably didn't even know about the fall.

He walked back inside the building and finished his shift in silence. He wanted to tell Hector, to tell somebody, but he was certain they would not believe him. He thought somebody must have seen it, from a window or something. But no one said a word.

That night in his apartment, he fretted about what to do. Should he call the police? No crime was committed. The media? He had no proof.

He resolved to talk to Dr. Finley. Yes, Dr. Finley must be informed about this. He would know what to do. Michael trusted his boss's judgment. He hoped he could find the time to arrange an appointment in the administrator's busy schedule, because he did not want to wait.

Michael did not have to wait at all.

The next morning in his mail cubby he found a note saying that Dr. Finley wanted to see him in his office right away, at 8:00.

He was ushered into the spacious oak-paneled office that he had not been in since the day he was hired. Finley, a balding, bespectacled man of sixty, sat at his desk in front of the tall casement windows with their splendid view of the grounds. "Good morning, Michael. Have a seat."

Dr. Finley closed the folder he had been perusing, looked at Michael, and said, "Do you like working here?"

"Sure."

"Are you satisfied with your pay and benefits?"

Michael felt a little puzzled, but said, "Yes."

"Do the people here treat you OK?"

"Yeah, they're fine. Why?"

"Then is it fair to say you'd like to keep your job here?"

Michael looked nervously around the room. "What do you mean? Am I in trouble? What did I do?"

Dr. Finley raised his hand. "Nothing. Not yet anyway."

"Well, what is this about, then?"

"Michael, I'd like you to meet someone."

Michael's eyes widened as he saw a man walk in from the adjoining office, a man with well-barbered salt-and-pepper hair, dressed in a tailored suit and knit tie. It was Mr. Barnes. He said, "Hello, Michael. Pleased to meet you."

Michael stared at the man, his mouth agape. "But…but…I saw you. You're…a bunch of wires and relays and…you're a robot!"

"No, Michael, I assure you, I am flesh and blood, just like you." He extended his hand to shake, and Michael grasped it. It felt warm and fleshy. He could feel bone and muscle underneath the skin. He looked into Mr. Barnes' eyes and saw life and intelligence. He looked closely at the portion of Mr. Barnes' neck extending out from his dress shirt collar. He could see no tear, no scar, no evidence of any cut or repair.

As Mr. Barnes sat down, Dr. Finley said, "Michael, Mr. Barnes is one of our most generous benefactors. Every year he writes us a check with a great many zeroes on it. His generosity is the principal reason the accommodations in our rooms are so pleasant, why our staff is first-rate, why medical care is second to none, why our food is good, and on and on."

"I am the director of the TechnoGen Institute. Perhaps you've heard of it."

"But....but...he's a real man? He's not a robot?" Michael's brow furrowed, and he asserted, "I know what I saw. I saw a damaged robot!"

"Technically, it wasn't a robot, Michael," Mr. Barnes said. "It was an android. He was developed at my institute. We call him Jerry. That's short for Geriatric Android Prototype. We were originally going to call him Humanitarian Artificial Life, but that unfortunately shortened to HAL."

"An android? You mean like Data on *Star Trek*?"

Mr. Barnes smiled. "You know, I enjoyed reruns of that show when I was little. But our version of Data was not just any android. It was programmed to look and act like me. Like the son in my mother's photo album, the one she dimly remembers, if at all."

"You mean all along, this thing was visiting her? Pretending to be you?"

"Not all along. But for some time now."

"Dr. Finley, you *knew* about this robot, er, android?"

"Yes," Finley said. "We agreed to it as a trial."

"A trial for what?"

"Let me explain," Mr. Barnes said, leaning forward on the table and interlacing his fingers. "Michael, you haven't been here very long, but you've undoubtedly noticed that people who suffer from Alzheimer's and other dementia go through a particular form of hell. It's so gradual that it sneaks up on them. At first, they don't remember little things. Last night's supper. The names of friends. But then before long they don't remember the names of their grandchildren, or their children, or the person they were married to for forty years. Little by little, everything they remember is chipped away, erased. You have these people who look and talk like the parent, the wife, the husband you've known your whole life, but whose memories of their entire lives are gone. It gets to the point where they don't know who you are any more. Even if you visit every week. They don't even know who they are. When a person's memory goes, everything that person is or was or can be is taken away. What's left is a shell—a body that could go on living for years, but inside that shell is a person who just exists, lives day to day, eats and sleeps and talks with the people around her, but has no other life in any sense."

He continued, "Modern medical advances have allowed us to keep the body alive and functioning longer. Ironically, some of the technological advancements my own company has made have resulted in greater longevity for the elderly. But we still cannot prevent or cure this terrible affliction.

"And what of the families?" he continued. "You've watched them, Michael. It is extremely difficult for families to go through the pain of continuing to visit these people week after week, month after month, knowing that their loved ones have stopped recognizing them or remembering them.   Many relatives become impatient and frustrated, and some simply give up and stop coming. But when they do, they are often wracked with guilt, feeling that they are coldly abandoning their loved ones to the mercy of an institution.

"Their only other option, though, is to continue to visit long after the disease has taken its toll.   So they face the prospect of years of uncomfortable visits, sitting here for awkward periods of empty smiles and silences. Having to take time out of their busy lives to make the journey to visit someone who in all likelihood will not remember them the next day.   Parading young grandchildren before an old woman who was never a grandmother to them, never anyone other than a kindly old lady sitting in a chair in the visitors' room."

"Yes, sir," Michael allowed. "I imagine it's very painful."

"Painful to watch, and even more agonizing to experience, son," Mr. Barnes added.   "It's a situation I found myself in when my mother was diagnosed and had to be put in this home. I tried to come and visit her regularly, but as time wore on, she recognized me less and less until, inevitably, I just became that nice man that stops to see her.

"I may be a successful engineer and the head of a large institute, but I am as weak and frail as the next guy when it comes to things like this.   I became increasingly frustrated and impatient with my mother's inability to remember simple things. Again and again I was short with her.   And it became increasingly difficult to arrange to visit her on any regular basis. It's a two-hour drive one way from my offices, and I can seldom afford that much time away. I am usually swamped with meetings most weeks, and it's getting to the point where three or four months of the year I have to be in Europe or Asia. I began to ask myself, as I suspect nearly every family in this situation does, why it mattered whether I kept visiting her or not. If she didn't remember me anyway, what was the point? But then I kept coming back to something."

"What was that?"

Mr. Barnes smiled and paused for emphasis. "Have you watched the clients when someone comes to visit, Michael? Have you noticed how cheered up most of them get? Even if they don't recognize the visitor, they are happy to see someone, anyone. It breaks up their long, monotonous days. The fact that they do not remember the visit for very long afterward does not seem to matter to them. They seem to know when they are visited, and when they are not."

Michael said, "Yes, they always like visits."

"When I thought about that, I hit upon a very practical solution."

"A robot visitor?" Michael said. "But how…how could that possibly…."

"Possibly work?" Barnes said. "My institute has been working on cutting-edge android technology for some time. We'd been looking for some practical ways to test their performance. Our people did detailed studies of my walk, my mannerisms, my gestures. I spent hours recording thousands of words and phrases, which our language algorithm could formulate into responses for almost any question it might be asked. But we'd had language and motion-copying technology for some time. The real challenge was in getting the look right—the skin color and texture, the eyes, the mouth. We're always working on improving that."

Michael was astonished. "And you just…substituted this thing for yourself? Just like that?"

Barnes shook his head. "No, in gradual steps. We sent it in one week, then I came the next to see whether Mother remembered it. And then we sent it in again a few weeks later. I visited her when I could, but gradually, it stood in for me most of the time. Staff tells me she never seemed to notice, or care."

Michael sat back in his chair to absorb all of this for a moment. Then he said, "But, Dr. Finley, is this deception OK with you? What if somebody found out about this?"

"Everybody on the floor knows, Michael."

"They do?"

Dr. Finley nodded slowly.

Barnes leaned in and lowered his voice. "Michael," he said, "Jerry is not the only android visitor."

"What!?"

"There are at least two more regular visitors to patients here who are our androids."

Dr. Finley added, "And you've seen them. But you can't tell, can you?"

Michael was stunned. No, he hadn't been able to tell.

He struggled for words. "But, but, it's inhuman! It's— "

"Is it, Michael?" Barnes cut in. "You watch the floor next time. You look at how happy those old people are to be visited. Look at how their faces light up. You see how pleased they are that someone—or something—took the time to brighten up their lonely hours for a little while. And, I reiterate, they won't know."

"That is," Dr. Finley noted, "unless somebody spills the beans. Which brings us to the real purpose of this meeting."

Michael glanced nervously from one man to the other.

Dr. Finley continued, "I've had this conversation with almost everyone we've hired. They all maintain a bond of silence. Nobody speaks of it. We want you to promise, to swear, to do the same. If you decide to stay on with us, under these conditions, we're prepared to give you a ten percent increase in salary immediately, and a twenty-five percent increase after six months of satisfactory work. And a very generous medical and dental plan, better than you'd get anywhere else."

"In exchange for my silence?"

"Yes."

"But what if I think this is monstrous? What if I take it to the media?"

Mr. Barnes smiled, his lip and brow tinged with just the slightest bit of condescension. "Now think about that, Michael. For one thing, no one would believe you. And if they came around to check, they would not find any androids. We can simply stop sending them in at a moment's notice."

"But that's not the point," Dr. Finely broke in. "The point is that we have the beginnings of something rather special going on here. We have an arrangement that benefits everyone. The clients are visited regularly to stave off their loneliness, and the distraught families can be relieved of their guilt for no longer wanting to tolerate the painful visits to their loved ones. Everybody wins."

Dr. Finley paused a moment to let it sink in and then said, "Is that so monstrous?"

Wednesday, two o'clock. Another bright, sunny day. The common room was immaculate. Michael watched the visitors parade in and take their places at the tables and in the plush chairs, greeting their loved ones with smiles and upbeat voices.

Mr. Barnes, in his tailored suit and well-barbered hair, sat erect in his chair and said, "Hello, Mother. How are you today? I'm your son Alan." She smiled, nodded hesitantly, and began to reply to his questions.

Across the room, Mrs. Gonzales had a visitor today, to whom she could grouse on end. Mrs. Adams kept repeating to her visitor, "Now, who are you, again?" The visitor smiled and went on, pleasantly even-tempered.

The dozen or so visitors asked their loved ones about their days, their meals, their morning's activities. Sometimes they got answers to their questions, though often they got vague responses, or mere pleasantries, or confused looks. It did not seem to matter.

Michael surveyed the room, picking up snatches of the conversations:

"When can I go home?"

"We're having lasagna today."

"Look what I made."

"Oh, the pains come and go."

And over the intervals of hesitant or rambling responses from their aunts and uncles and grandmothers, the unruffled visitors exchanged their small talk, held their smiles, and nodded amiably.

The room was as cheery as the sunlight streaming in through the tall windows. All the visitors today seemed so kindly, Michael thought. So patient.

And he smiled. It was all good.

Afterword to "Jerry"

This is the second story I've done about Alzheimer's and dementia, after "The Corners of My Mind." But it's not that I'm particularly obsessed with that topic. This story came about through the idea of robots.

I'd been reading a volume of Ray Bradbury short stories, and I enjoyed his *Martian Chronicles* story about the robot family on Mars (which reminds me of the *Twilight Zone* story with similar theme). Then *CBS Morning News* did a piece on robots, followed by a tongue-in-cheek bit about how it would be easy to make and program fuzzy-animal robots to be people's companions and get people to care about them. Then it hit me—caring robots!

CBS Morning News also did a piece on a man who visits his Alzheimer's-stricken wife every week, even though she doesn't recognize him and just lives from day to day, moment to moment. Then the PBS *Nova scienceNOW* series did a segment on Feb. 23, 2011, about advanced developments in robot technology to make them more lifelike, including talking to people and responding. I watched that going, "That's my story!"

Out of Time

Trevor Matheson gazed up at the muted white ten-story building looming in front of him. The huge logo, its luminescent blue lettering visible from a mile away, read "TTT Institute."

He entered the spacious, glassy lobby and took the elevator up to the third floor reception. He strode across the impressive space to the secretary at the desk, a pert redhead whose name tag read "Gloria" and stated his business.

She took his name and entered some data into her console. "You're familiar with the procedure?" she asked.

"Yes, I've done this before."

She smiled. "I recognize you, Mr. Matheson. But I have to ask. Will this be for the hour?"

"Yes."

"Four hundred credits, please." He handed her his credit card, and she ran it.

She tapped some more entries into her console and then handed him a plastic ticket and said, "Room number four, down the hall and on the right."

He walked down the starkly clean ivory hallway to the room and swiped his ticket through the reader to enter. In front of him was a small console and a padded chair. He sat down and inserted his ticket into the activation slot. The touch screen on the console in front of him read, "Enter the desired location, date, year, and local time." He entered the data. It then instructed him to don his helmet and connect it. He picked up the smooth metallic blue viewing helmet, connected the cord, and lowered the visor. He took a breath, and then he tapped the start button. He felt a surge of energy, as if some giant machinery had just whoomed into operation in a nearby room, which might be exactly what happened.

Before him appeared a distorted, spotty blue image that pixilated into the logo of TTT and then formed into a disclaimer statement. He had read it before and knew what it said. Time Travel Technologies, Inc., was not responsible for any reaction or consequence that may ensue as a result of his viewing these images, blah, blah, blah. He glazed over most of it, waiting for it to finish. *Yeah, I get it*, he thought, *the truth is the truth. History is history. I know what I'm asking for*.

The image blurred and then suddenly became clear. Startlingly clear. He saw his old college studio apartment from his junior year. He saw the poster on the wall he had almost forgotten. He saw the shelves with books and notebooks. He heard his stereo playing. He saw the tiny kitchen cluttered with dishes and coffee cups. He had forgotten how he hadn't taken the time to clean up that night, not knowing whether she would come over.

And then he saw her, sitting on the couch, finishing her wine. Alison. Once again, after so many years, he heard her voice. He watched as his own gangly and much thinner twenty-year-old self walked over to her, poured her some more wine, and asked her if she had liked the movie. He could again taste the wine that he had forty years before. They talked about the movie for a while, longer than he remembered they did. Actually, he had to admit he didn't remember much of what they talked about that night.

He watched himself make his move. First the kiss—long, slow, deeply felt. As his younger self kissed her, he could feel her lips warm and soft. The kissing went on for some time. He smelled her subtle perfume.   Then came the undoing of her blouse buttons, then the decorative belt on her skirt. She did not resist.   Trevor watched as his doppelganger asked her, "How about if I pull the bed out?"   She chuckled a little at his artlessness and said, "Sure."

He watched as the hide-a-bed was pulled out of the sofa.   He watched as she left for the bathroom, returning wearing only her bra and panties.   And he watched as the lovemaking commenced, hesitant and unsure at first, then with more ardor.

He could see every inch of her body that he wanted to see.   And he could feel it! He could feel her skin all over again as his young, unpracticed hand caressed her.   He could feel her soft blond hair.   He could feel her hands on his back.   His breathing increased.   He could feel his own tumescence. Every sensation. Incredible!

And suddenly it was over. The screen went black. His hour was up. The screen read, "Please remove your helmet and exit the chamber.   You may pay for additional time at the reception desk if you wish to view more.   Thank you for your patronage."

Trevor returned to his apartment in a jolly mood. He picked up the photo of his wife, now dead five years, and kissed it, saying, "You're next, my dear." He picked up the adjacent photo of his daughter, now thirty, and said, "Maybe your first word, sweetie, or your first step, eh?"

He sat in his favorite chair and ruminated over the events in his life. *Oh, yeah*, he thought, *I've got plenty of material.*

The following night, Trevor treated himself to scotch at the tavern, rather than the cheap beer he usually drank. He felt giddy. He said to his old friend sitting next to him, "I'm telling you, Roy, you gotta try time travel—it's great."

"So you really did it?" Roy asked.

"Yep. Paid the money."

"What'd you see?"

"Revisited my old college days. It was just like being there." Then, catching himself, he chuckled. "Well, I *was* there, actually."

Roy was two years older than Trevor, two years closer to anticipated retirement from their jobs as assemblers at the munitions plant. Roy was taller, and his face was leaner and more angular than Trevor's ruddy and rounded look, but they shared many things—graying hair, advancing arthritis, widower status, married daughters with families far away, and thus a need for companionship.

They also shared (and often groused about) limited finances. Their jobs were satisfying and paid reasonably well, but the high cost of living kept their apartments small and lifestyles modest.

Consequently, Roy asked, "Doesn't it cost a lot?"

"Four hundred credits for one hour."

Roy let out a low whistle. "That's damn expensive."

Trevor said, "For that you get to visit up to three different events. Or just stick with one."

"But I don't get it. How can they even do that?"

"I don't know. The TTT building is huge, and you only get to see a little part of it when you go there. I don't know what's in the rest of it. But does it matter? I mean, you don't have to know how your vehicle or your computer works in order to use it and enjoy it. Somebody figured it out. That's good enough for me."

"So you can go anywhere?" Roy asked, sipping his beer.

"It's not really a where," Trevor said. "It's a when. We're going to have to come up with new language to describe this. You can go any*when*." He chuckled at his inventiveness.

"You mean you can go back and see historical events, anything?"

"Oh, yeah, people can go and see anything any time now. Gloria the receptionist tells me that the great historical events are really popular, like Lincoln's assassination, or Kennedy's, or the signing of the Declaration of Independence. Or Woodstock. Whatever."

Roy shook his head and stared at his glass. "That's incredible."

"It's revolutionized our understanding of history. And we've had to revise some long-held beliefs, too.   She tells me that people get really shocked, even angry, when they see what Christ really looked like.   Some want their money back. And some of them want to see the Garden of Eden, or Noah's Ark. As if they could."

"And this thing puts you right there? So you can really see and hear it?"

"Yep. You're actually there. And when you go back to witness an experience of your own in your lifetime, there's an added bonus. You get to feel what you felt then. All over again."

"You mean, if you go back and watch yourself eat a meal, you taste the food?"

"You taste the food, smell it, feel the sensation of being full, everything.   It has something to do with stimulating the memory engrams of your brain."

A moment of silence. Roy took a sip, and then a devilish smile formed on his face. "So if you go back and watch yourself make love, do you…?"

Trevor smiled and nodded. "Yup. You got it."

"Whoa," Roy said. "That's like pornography."

Trevor shook his head. "How can it be porn when it's your own life? I mean, you've already lived it once. You're just experiencing it again."

"Boy," Roy said, taking a sip. "That just seems, I dunno, weird."

"You talk as though you don't know about the Institute," Trevor said.   "It's been around for, oh, three-four years now. Haven't you heard about this?"

"Well, I guess I heard some people talk. But I'm too goddamn busy to read the news. And most of the people I hang with, well, they can't afford that kind of stuff."

"Start saving your money. It's so worth it."

"So what historical events are you gonna see?"

"I haven't looked at anything historical yet. I've stuck with events from my own life."

"You just want to revisit your own life?"

"Well, yeah, parts of it. The good parts."

"Don't you remember them?"

"Oh, you'd be surprised what you forget. We always think our memory is so vivid, but it's really pretty subjective. Besides, some parts are really fun to relive."

"But you can't talk to people in the past, right?"

Trevor shook his head. "You can't actually interact. You're just a witness. You're looking through this sorta shield or force field, which allows you to experience what's going on. So you're not really there. Well, you are, but you aren't. But what you see is actually what happened. It's like you're watching the world's greatest, most incredibly realistic TV show."

"And you can't change anything?"

"No. That's what you have to get used to. We always heard about this idea from Einstein and those guys that time travel was impossible. That's been turned on its head. And so has the whole time travel paradox question."

"Paradox?"

"You must have heard of it. The logical problem that says that if somebody goes back in time and interacts with people or even with nature, he'll change the future, our present. But if our present isn't changed, then nobody could have ever changed it."

"Huh?"

"The example they always give is like if you went back in time and met your grandfather as a young man, before he got married and had children, and got into an argument with him, and killed him. You would never have been born. But you were born, so you couldn't possibly do that. Nobody could prevent Lincoln's assassination because it happened. It couldn't suddenly not happen."

"So there's no danger of changing history?"

"No, that's the beauty of it. When these guys finally cracked the mystery of time travel, finally found out how to open a portal to the past, they found out that this shield or whatever it is allows us to experience past events, but separated from them. It's not like a doorway, more like a window. We can't interact with the past, so we can't change it. But we can go back and watch it as much as we want."

"And so now we know exactly how all of history happened?"

"Well, they haven't exactly done all the research yet. They have guys working on that. But the kicker is that somebody figured out that this technology could be used for entertainment. Ordinary folks like you and me can go in, pay the money, and visit any event we want. It pays for the research. Like I say, you really ought to try it."

Roy finished his drink and, like the curmudgeon he often was, said, "Well, just don't come to me for money when you've spent your last credit revisiting your fifth birthday party."

"My fifth birthday party wasn't that great." Trevor held up a finger. "But my twenty-first— now *that* was a party!"

The following week, Trevor visited TTT again, to stare intently at a simple scene of a woman cradling an infant in her arms.

He remembered so very little about his mother, dead in a vehicle crash when he had been only six. He had photos, of course, but he barely recalled what she looked or sounded or felt like. But there she was—her soft brown hair, her soothing voice, her bright green eyes, smiling and cooing at him. He could feel her fingers running across his infant self's cheek. He could *feel* her! Tears began to well in his eyes. At that moment, nothing could be more satisfying to him.

That night, his mind roved over other possibilities. He thought about revisiting his wedding day, but he felt he remembered that well enough. But his daughter—ah, that was a curious patchwork of memories. He remembered bits and pieces of her growing up, but felt gaps. The day of her birth was clear enough in his memory. But when was her first word, exactly? He wasn't sure. Her first step? Oh, to relive those! Her first Christmas? No, she would have been too young to make that worth revisiting. But maybe the glee of her fourth Christmas? The one where his wife did such a nice job cooking the goose? He could enjoy that all over again.

Two weeks later Trevor ran into Roy at the tavern again. To his surprise, Roy said, "You look terrible. Where ya been?" Roy stared at his friend's sallow eyes and haggard expression. "You've been going to the Institute, haven't you?"

"Uh, sometimes, yeah," Trevor said.

"We haven't seen you at work in three days. What, are you just reliving the past over and over again?"

"Oh, but you don't understand. It's so great. I went back to my honeymoon. And I relived our whole family trip out west twenty years ago."

"So if it was so great, why do you look so downcast?"

Trevor mumbled something about not knowing what he meant.

Roy pressed. "How are you paying for all this?"

"What business is it of yours?"

"Well, I couldn't help but notice that I haven't seen you wear a new shirt or pants in, well, quite a while. And I don't see you wearing that nice watch you used to have. What happened to it? And I happen to know you moved to a smaller apartment."

"So what?"

"So are you strapped for money?"

"Well, yes, all right, I'm having a little cash flow problem. Nothing that won't keep till the next pay cycle."

"You're spending all your money on time travel jaunts, aren't you?"

"No! I'm not!"

"Don't BS me, Trevor. It's all you've talked about for weeks."

"Well, what if I am? I'm learning a great deal. I told you time travel is a terrific experience. You ought to try it. Once you try it, you're hooked."

"You make it sound like a drug."

"It's not a drug! It's education. It's feeding your brain."

"Just reliving your life's moments over and over?"

"That's not all I'm doing!"

"What's that old Jefferson Airplane line? 'Feed your head?'"

"You know what? Shut up! Just shut up!" Trevor rose from the stool and stormed out.

He seethed. He seethed at Roy's ignorance. He seethed at his own inability to defend what he was doing, when it seemed perfectly reasonable to him. Beneficial, really. Why couldn't Roy see that?

But now he had no one to talk to. If Roy didn't understand, no one else would, either.

He thought about asking Gloria out. But she was half his age. Then he thought about going back into her past to learn more about her, but he gave up on that idea, too.

The idea had been nagging at him for weeks, ever since he first revisited the images of his mother. His father had told him the story of how his mother had died in a car crash. He vaguely remembered the pain, the confusion, the anxiety of that time, but to his six-year-old mind, it had all been a swirl. He was sure there had been things they had not told him. And no, he never wanted to revisit the crash. But where was she going that day? To the doctor, he had always been given to understand. But for what? He never knew. And there was no doctor's office that he recalled in the part of town where the crash occurred.

As days passed, his curiosity egged him on. On his next visit to TTT, he settled the helmet onto his head and carefully programmed the settings for the date of the crash, but earlier in the day. He fine-tuned the settings until the image he wanted appeared—his mother, in the vehicle, driving. He followed as she drove down a street unfamiliar to him. Was this his home town? He was not sure. She drove into a driveway, got out, and walked up to a second-floor apartment. A man let her in. She fell into the man's arms. They embraced. They kissed. He had never seen the man before, or since. But at that moment Trevor wanted to kill him. He had to stop watching, even though his time was not up. He could not go on.

His mother had been cheating on his father. And on him, too.

The pain was wrenching. He threw off his helmet. He slammed his clenched fist on the counter top. That sweet, kind woman, about whom he had heard nothing but good from everyone who knew her, had a dark secret. Did they know? Did his father know?

He stopped going to TTT for a while. But only for a while.

Two weeks later, Trevor found himself once again staring intently at the screen. His breath caught in his throat. His heart raced. His palms sweated. Agonizingly slowly, almost as if in slow motion, he watched Perry Smith fire the shotgun blasts that killed the Kansas farm family—first Mr. Clutter, then his son Kenyon. Then he half ran, half stumbled upstairs to shoot Mrs. Clutter, then finally Nancy, who screamed when he came in. As her scream was silenced by the blast, Trevor felt the gore rise in his throat. He couldn't stay. Tearing the helmet off, he dashed out of the room and down the hall to the rest room. He burst through the door and headed for the nearest stall, barely reaching the toilet a moment before he threw up.

"What was I thinking?" he wondered. *"Why did I pick that to watch?"*

He vomited some more and then raised his head up to wait for the queasiness to pass.

He muttered aloud, "What's wrong with me? What have I become?"

He tried to stay away. He managed to stay away three weeks. He took a second job and saved his money. But then he went back. And kept going.

Visit after visit, hour after hour, day after day, the images flowed in front of him and swirled in his mind, assaulting his senses—

February 13, 1483: Tomas De Torquemada sentencing a weeping man to his death in a Valencia court, watching him being dragged away as he protests his innocence

September 22, 1692: Eight women hanging in the public square in Salem, Massachusetts, condemned as witches

October 1, 1943: The great, oily gray locomotive chugging to a halt at the Auschwitz gate and the uniformed troops herding the anxious and confused deportees off the cattle cars

February 14, 1929: Machine guns rattling and a haze of blue smoke filling the air as seven members of the North Side Gang crumple on the floor of the warehouse at Dickens and Clark in Chicago

June 26, 1876: General George Armstrong Custer's 7th Cavalry being overwhelmed and massacred by Lakota and Cheyenne warriors at Little Big Horn

Each week he pursued more and more dark dates in history, more and more gut-wrenching images to wallow in, testing the limits of his empathy and his tolerance for pain.

He struggled through many fevered, sleepless nights and tense, agitated days. He tried staying away from the Institute, but he found himself inexorably pulled back. He read books and papers on historical events to research possible visits. He went without meals to save up credits. He lied to people about visits to museums or movies to conceal where he went.

He was the moth drawn to the flame. He could not stop.

But it had to stop, somehow. He knew what Roy would say if he talked to Roy, which he hardly did any more. Roy would say, "You got a problem, you fix it."

Yes, fix it. But how?

Until one day at the munitions factory he stumbled, almost by accident, upon a solution. In a flash of inspiration, he knew what he had to do.

He was back for the third time that week. But this time he selected something interesting but innocuous—the New York World's Fair of 1939. He let the images of crowds and exhibits unreel before him, but he only half paid attention. At length, he removed from his jacket pocket a small device, hardly bigger than his wallet. He set it down upon the counter top in front of the console and activated a switch. A tiny green light popped on. It was ready.

He came out of the booth. "You didn't take very long this time," Gloria said in her usual cheery manner. "I think you have more time left."

"Gloria," he said, "get out of the building! Leave now!"

"What?" she responded, confused.

"Just go!" he urged. Then he looked up and exhorted to the array of desks and cubicles across the room, "Everybody. Get out. Now! I think there's a fire or something!" He waited a moment for her to get up and leave. He saw that some workers rose from their desks or offices, though others just gaped in disbelief.

He turned and headed down a small corridor that he had scoped out in earlier visits. It led only to a utility closet and a freight elevator, and thus no one was around. When he passed the red metal fire alarm box on the wall, he jabbed it with his elbow, and as the alarm sounded, he hustled along to the door leading to the elevator. He took the freight elevator down to the main floor, reasoning that everyone trained in fire drill procedures would take the stairs.

He arrived at the street level and ducked out of a side door into an alley. As he had suspected, no one was there. From there, he walked casually out onto the street and across to another block. He turned back toward the main entrance of the

Institute building to see frightened workers pouring out of the exits, screaming and panicky, the fire alarm buzzing raucously from out of the windows.

He waited many moments, until people no longer emerged and it appeared as though the building had been evacuated. Then he turned and began to walk away. As he did so, he pulled from his pocket a tiny transmitter and pressed a button on it.

The third floor exploded with a thunderous boom. Vehicles and awnings and traffic signs rattled on the street, and shattered glass from broken windows sprinkled over the length of the block. Behind him, he could hear the shouts and screams from onlookers.

He felt good. He felt free, liberated, as if a great burden had been lifted from his shoulders.

His only regret was that he would never be able to go back to relive it and enjoy the sensation all over again.

Afterword to "Out of Time"

I love time travel stories.

From Ray Bradbury's "Sound of Thunder" to *The Twilight Zone* to *Back to the Future* to *Looper* to *12 Monkeys* to Stephen King's *11/22/63*, and on and on. I have enjoyed how the intriguing concept has been dealt with again and again in so many varied and imaginative ways.

And that was my problem. I wanted to do something with time travel, but I felt it had been done so much. How could the idea be treated differently?

The stickler was always the Paradox. Basically, you're up against a wall when you write a story about going back in time and trying to change something or avoid something from being changed. It can't be changed, because it hasn't been changed.

I wondered about writing a time travel story that gets around the Paradox. What if we could visit the past, but not affect it by our visit? So that we could go anywhere and see anything? What possibilities would that open up? I found that idea appealing, and this story is an exploration of some perhaps unintended consequences of that capability.

The Cup of Conlaoch

ary Finnegan braked her bicycle to a stop on the gravel road that crested the great hill and paused to gaze out upon the Irish seacoast below. She admired the rugged beauty of the coastline. The salty breeze ruffled her auburn hair, the midday sun playing off her tresses in streaks of gold. If she gave the sun its druthers, it would burnish her fair skin with its dusting of freckles. But she never stayed out long enough for that.

She watched the slate-colored waves roiling and pounding the shore two hundred yards below. She noted, as she often had, that from the wind and the waves, the sloping landscape had been scooped and whittled away over the centuries. The erosion had been so gradual, of course, that one could not see it, but she thought that in her childhood twenty years ago, the craggy hill had been smoother and extended a little farther out toward the sea. Old men in the village had told her as much. Rocks and even boulders that she did not remember from childhood poked out and dotted the hillside.

She glanced at her watch. Yes, time to return to the village already. She turned her bicycle onto the road and pushed off. But the front wheel wobbled in the loose gravel on the shoulder as she tried to pump to get up some speed. Before she could get rolling, the front wheel angled, and the bicycle turned itself and headed down the slope from the road. Mary let out a gasp and braked frantically, skidding, but her front wheel hit a solid rock poking out of the ground. The bicycle pitched over, and she was flung headlong onto the ground ten feet down the slope from the road.

She mumbled a curse at her luck, not just for falling but for soiling her good slacks. Her mother would have a word or two to say about that.

And how would her father react? With the edge in his voice and the wink in his eye, it might be: "Forgotten how to ride a bicycle now, have ye?" Or perhaps: "Well, isn't it a good thing that we can't afford a car, then? Lord knows where that would end up!"

She had his biting wit to look forward to.

She felt pain and some moistness in her leg. She pulled up her pant leg and looked. Sure enough, she had scraped herself. And with only her handkerchief to dab on it. She then turned to look back up the slope a few feet where her bicycle lay and noticed the scratches.

She turned to get up but stumbled on a patch of loose soil, dislodging about a bucketful and losing her balance in the bargain. Disgusted, she sat there a moment and looked out once again at the sea. "So much for enjoying the view," she grumbled.

As she turned to rise once again, more carefully this time, she noticed something poking out of the ground. "Well, what have we here?" she wondered.

She pulled the object out. It was squat and round, rather like a cup or shallow bowl, about four inches across, and encrusted with dirt and grime.

"So, a scraped leg and a gouged fender, and this is what I've got to show for it?" she grumbled.

On a whim, she stuck it in her jacket pocket, and then managed to right her bicycle and pedal the three miles back to the village of Cragardh. She steered nimbly through the narrow streets, down Hill Street and through Main, right at Kelly, until the well-worn sign of Finnegan's Pub signaled that she was home.

The pub was nearly empty at this time of day, early afternoon. Its usual patrons who had jobs were working now, and those who were retired were undoubtedly resting up. The peat fireplace in the corner was cold and ashen. The sunlight streaming through the stained glass windows revealed too much dust.

Mary's father Seamus Finnegan busied himself behind the bar. His ruddy Irish countenance that later would beam with laughter and joviality as he chatted with his customers was now tight-lipped and a bit grim as he focused on tallying receipts and sorting invoices.

"And where have you been?" he asked, barely looking up as she walked in.

"I've been biking up on the hilltop. It's beautiful there today."

"Yer late."

"You told me to start at one. It's—"

"It's a quarter past. And that makes ye late." He looked at his daughter as she removed her jacket and smoothed down her breeches a bit to try to conceal her injury, unsuccessfully.

"And what happened to ye, then?" he asked her.

She told him.

"So you think maybe the law of gravity doesn't work up on the seaside, do ye?" That was a new one on her.

"I'm all right, thanks for asking, and the bike just got a little scratch." She sat down at the end of the bar. She pulled the artifact out of her coat pocket and held it up to the light, adding, "And I found this half buried in the dirt nearby. What do you suppose it is? And how do you suppose it got there?"

Seamus glanced at it for a second and sniffed, "I suppose it's a piece of junk. And I suppose somebody chucked it away because they had no use for it. And while we're doin' all this supposin', d'ye suppose that side room will sweep itself out today, or d'ye suppose ye could get a broom and give it a bit of a hand?"

Her father's language had a musical lilt to it even when he was upbraiding her.

As Seamus turned to tend to the bar, Mary held the object up to the light and scrutinized it, running her fingers over the surface and gently knocking some dirt from it. She exposed some odd-shaped lines and figures inscribed along the side. "Look," she said. "It's got some sort of writing or characters on it."

"Mary Kathleen Finnegan! Will ye put that thing away now and get on with yer chores before the evening roosh commences!" The lilt had gone out of his voice.

☩   ☩   ☩   ☩   ☩   ☩

The girl sat atop the crest of the hill and stared up at the moon, brilliant and nearly full in the clear night sky. She drank in the scent of the ocean breeze and watched the rolling waves far below, their undulating peaks basking in the moonlight. She pulled her goatskin tighter around her shoulders to ward off the cooling night air.

Suddenly, she heard a rustling off in the brush. She whirled around and looked to her right.

"Arlana?" she heard.

"Conlaoch?¹" she whispered back.

From out of the brush appeared a young man, tall, with dark shaggy hair and fledgling beard, clad in skins and leggings. They looked at each other for a moment.

She got up and rushed to him. Their arms encircled.

"You came," she said.

"Did you not think I would be here?" he answered.

"I never know whether you will come until you do."

"Fear not," he said. "Something very strong would have to stop me."

They sat upon the ground and looked at the moon and the ocean. For many minutes, they did not speak.

She broke the silence by simply saying, "The fishing has been bad lately."

"Yes, in my village, too," he replied. "We are hungry."

"The priest and the old men think it is an omen."

"They think everything is an omen."

"Maybe it is," he said. "The gods are mysterious in their ways."

---

¹ *pron.* KON-la

"I do not think I believe in omens," she said after a moment. "If everything is an omen, then nothing is."

"Don't you believe in the gods?"

She paused for a moment, then said, "Look at the night sky. Do you know what the stars are? How they got there?"

"My priest tells us that they are jewels scattered by the gods," Conlaoch said.

"But how does he know?"

"What do you mean, how does he know? He is the priest."

"Why does that mean he knows?" she said. "He is just a man. Born in the village, like you. And he passes on the things others before him have told him."

Conlaoch frowned. "I don't know about your village priest, but ours is a good man. He is a healer. His knowledge of herbs and poultices is amazing. We need him."

"Yes, my village priest is a good man, too," she replied. "But I do not think he knows more about the sky than the next man."

"You have quite a mind for one so young."

"So I am too much for you?"

He smiled. "You are just right for me."

He embraced her, and they sat for many minutes on the hillside.

"I cannot stay long," she said. "I will be missed."

"I will, too," he said. "When can I see you again?"

"I will try to come in two nights, if there is no rain. The moon will be full, to guide our way. But it is not easy. I must wait until the village is asleep, and it seems there is always a noisy goat or crying child."

"I will wait," he said softly, looking into her dark eyes.

Arlana crept very quietly back into the low-ceilinged dugout cavern in the hillside that was her home, making sure to route herself from the direction of the village latrine. She scurried under the cover of the pelts on her bier in the corner and tried to lie motionless.

A moment later, from the supine figure under a heap of pelts on the opposite side of the space came the voice of her mother saying, "Where were you?"

"At the latrine."

"You were gone for a long time."

"I was out walking on the hills for a while."

"That's dangerous. Don't do that."

"I'm hungry. Is there anything to eat?"

"There might be a leftover oat cake."

"Is that all?"

Oat cakes, gruel, and water. All that there had been for many days. No wonder the men felt the poor fishing was a curse, she thought.

The restless bleating of one of the goats outside made her think about how much she would like some roasted goat. But no goats could be killed for months, at least until the winter, because the males could still sire and the females could still give milk for the young ones in the village.

"We're all hungry, dear," her mother said softly. " Tomorrow the priest will pray to the gods for a better catch. Until then, go to sleep."

✠   ✠   ✠   ✠   ✠   ✠

The pub was nearly full. The peat fire burned hot and smokeless in the old fireplace, warming a dozen folks who sat around it playing cards, swapping stories, and savoring their pints. Off in the corner, a session had just started up. Tonight it was uilleann pipes, two fiddles, a bodhran, and a tin whistle, along with the ever-present Old Finn, who clacked away with his battered kitchen spoons to the same beat whatever the tune, sucking on his old pipe and flashing his grizzled grin.

The main room was decorated, as so many Irish country pubs were, with wooden tables and chairs, painted and wainscoted walls, and a motley collection of antiques, knickknacks, and Guinness signs. On the east wall above the entrance to the side room, the main shelf housed the most prized of the family possessions, including Seamus' father's fiddle and his mother's tea kettle.

Seamus and his wife Eileen scurried back and forth behind the bar, she filling orders for sandwiches and cheese plates, he pulling pints and joking with the patrons. Mary wound her way from table to table taking orders and balancing trays of drinks, dodging outstretched legs and grabby hands.

Men in the pub wanted to dance with her, or maybe just talk with her, but they were all at least twenty years beyond her twenty-four. Most of them knew, at least in their sober moments, that they had no chance with her.   In the raucous, merry atmosphere of a typical pub night in an Irish village, she felt compelled to tread a fine line between being friendly and social, and keeping boundaries.

As she withstood the jokes and bawdy comments of the grizzled old patrons night after night, she had to face the grim realization that there were really no available men her age in the village. Six or seven years before, they had all gone off to do their duty and fight the Nazi menace, and none of them had come back, at least in one piece. Rare it was that a man younger than thirty came into the pub.

But tonight one did.

She noticed him about nine o'clock at the end of the bar. He was smartly dressed, sandy-haired, clean shaven, with a bright, engaging smile. Or so it seemed when he ordered a Guinness from her father. Mary had to move quickly. She hastily served the drinks on her tray and then scooted behind the bar. She sidled up to her father and said, "I'll get that one."

"Oh, will ye?" Seamus said, with his sardonic twinkle.

Mary took the filled pint glass and served it to the young man.

"Well, that's quite the service here," he said.

"You're new here."

"Can you tell?"

"I know everybody in the place. It's the same crowd every night. A new face stands out. Especially a face like yours." She smiled.

"Well," he blushed a bit at her forwardness, "you know how to make a chap feel welcome." He knew what she was doing. She didn't care.

"So where you from, then?" she asked, warmly.

"Well, I'm currently working out of Trinity College." He spoke in smooth, educated Dublin English. She loved the sound of it.

"Doing what?"

"I'm part of the team that's excavating the ruins out near the seacoast about three miles from here."

"Oh, I've seen those. It's an ancient village or something?"

"Right. This part of the country has been settled for tens of thousands of years. We've started to uncover the ruins of an ancient settlement."

"So you know about ancient ruins and

objects and things like that?"

"I'm an archaeologist. That's my specialty."

"You know, I found this thing earlier today." She retrieved it from the back shelf. "I dug it up out of the earth up at the crest of Cragardh Hill up on the coast road. Maybe you can tell me what it is?"

"Let's have a look at it." She handed it to him. He held it up to the light and scrutinized it, brushing dirt off its surface. "I can tell you it's pretty old," he commented.

"You mean, like a hundred years or so?"

"No, I mean more like eight or ten thousand years."

"Really?"

"Mary! Ye've got tables!" her father's voice shouted from down the bar.

"Can you wait a few minutes?"

"I've got a full Guinness," he volunteered.

She glanced down the bar and then said to him, "I'll be back."

She left to tend to her waitressing chores and returned ten minutes later to find him still poring over the cup.

"Well, I'm glad to see you didn't run off with it," she said.

"No," he smiled. She liked his gleaming blue eyes. "I'm Dennis, by the way. Dennis Flaherty."

"And I'm Mary," she replied with a smile.

"So I heard," he said. "This is a very interesting object you have here. The bottom surface is charred, as if it had been used to heat something over a fire.   And then there are these symbols."

"Can you tell what the symbols mean?"

"No, but they're probably runes."

"Ruins?   You mean like the ruins you're digging up?"

"No, runes," he said, trying to make the pronunciation distinct.   "Ancient characters, like letters. Symbols, really."

"What do they mean?"

"Well, I can't tell offhand. I'd have to run them against our key and see if we can come up with anything. Do you mind if I take this with me?"

"To do what? Study it?"

"Have some experts in Dublin study it."

"You'll return it, won't you?"

"Of course."

"Well, all right, I suppose. When will I get it back?"

"Oh, I'm not sure. A week or two."

"So you'll be back, then?"

"Definitely." He smiled and looked into her eyes. "Does that suit you?"

She smiled back. "Oh, it suits me just fine."

☩   ☩   ☩   ☩   ☩   ☩

Two nights later, when the moon was full and high in the sky, Arlana and Conlaoch sat again on the hill overlooking the sea, watching the rolling waves far below endlessly crest and crash onto the shore.

"*I made you something,*" *he said.   He removed an object from the folds of his robe and held it out for her.   It was squat and round, rather like a cup or shallow bowl, about four inches across, and it gleamed even in the moonlight from being newly polished.*

She took it and gazed lovingly at it. "It's beautiful. What is it?"

"It can be a dish or a drinking cup. Whatever you want."

"And you made this yourself?"

"Yes," he beamed.   "I've been learning metalwork. I can make an axe head and a knife blade. I saved my metal scraps and shavings for weeks, and when I had enough, I melted them down and cast it. See the carvings I put on it?"

She ran her fingers over the runic characters around the side.   "They're beautiful! What do they mean?"

"I made up symbols for you, and me, and the moon, and love. So that no matter what happens, you will always have a reminder of me, and of our moments together on these nights."

She gazed at it lovingly for a few moments. Then she furrowed her brow and said, "What do you mean, no matter what happens? Is something wrong?"

"No.   But you know, one day you may fancy someone in your village. You may want to stop seeing me."

She grunted. "There is no one in our village I like. The men are either too old, or they are too young. And they are crude and stupid. There is no one like you. None of them would ever think to make a thing like this cup, something beautiful, just as a gift."

"You love your parents, don't you?"

"My parents can be trying. My father objects to everything that does not involve getting work done, and my mother is afraid that everything is an omen and will bring bad luck."

He paused for a moment, unsure of how to react to her admission.

She looked deeply into his eyes and said, "Conlaoch, I want to spend my time with you. Do you want to spend your time with me?"

"We are spending out time together. Every month when the moon is full enough to guide our way here in the night without a torch."

"I do not mean only two or three times a month. And I do not mean only for a little while at night. I mean all the time. Would you not like to be with me all the time?"

"Yes," he said, without hesitation. "But how?"

"There is only one thing to do. Tell them. Tell them that we will join together. Ask the priest for his blessing, but if he will not give it, tell them we will be together anyway."

"And defy our parents and our villages?' he reacted. *"They will hate us."*

"You do not know that. Maybe they will accept. Do they not believe in love? We will never know if we do not try."

"But what if they do not accept us?" he asked.

"What do you want to do?"

"I do not know. I need to think about it."

"Will you? Will you think about it?" She gazed into his eyes.

"Every minute I'm away from you," he said.

☨   ☨   ☨   ☨   ☨   ☨

A week after they met, and the day after his second evening visit to the pub, Dennis drove Mary down to the ruins of the ancient village his team had been excavating and studying.

"Wow," was her first reaction as they drove up. She saw a wide expanse of excavation, covering at least six hundred yards square, dug out of the rocky hills. In addition to the bulldozer and backhoe crews, she saw a team of at least ten men and women digging or scratching away at the earth with hammers, picks, and brushes. Off to the side, a trailer had been set up for living quarters, and she also saw several tents and canopies set up, beneath which young men and women cleaned and catalogued artifacts.

The contours of the village that was emerging were nearly circular, and Mary noticed the beginnings of digs into adjoining chambers off a central area, as well as segments of walls and irregular mounds of rocks.

"It's a long, painstaking process," Dennis explained. "And we're just beginning to get an idea of what might be found here."

"We always knew there was something here," she said to him. "When I was a girl, we used to ride our bicycles out here and play on the rocks. But we never imagined what might be beneath them. This is incredible."

"Does this place have a name?" she said as they left his car and began to walk down to the site.

"As far as we know, it's called Carraighardh, which is Gaelic for 'rock hill,'" he said. "We think that your village, Cragardh, is a variation of that and was probably named after it."

They walked down into the excavated area, and he showed her the layout of the village. They stood in the center of the dig in an open space about twenty feet across. He explained, "The village is laid out like a wheel, and this is the hub. We're standing in what was probably the main gathering area, sort of like a village square. We found remnants of a fire pit in the center, and this is probably where they held their tribal councils and ceremonies. And over here is one of their living areas."

He turned and led her off into an opening in the hillside. "Watch your head," he said as he ducked down and walked through the cave-like entrance to the interior chamber.

"This is the first one of these chambers that we've excavated," he said. "We think we'll find many more as we dig around the circumference of the main area. This is probably where one family lived."

Mary looked around to see a vaguely circular space big enough to accommodate sleeping areas for several people, plus what looked to be a crude food preparation area off to one side. She also saw a fire pit in the center of the space. "The smoke probably rose through some sort of chimney opening in the roof, since covered over," Dennis explained.

"So this is how the early people of this country lived," he went on after she had looked around for several minutes. "Essentially a close-knit community, living in an arrangement of dug out caves for shelter. Probably relying on each other for all the things necessary for life."

Mary had a hundred questions. "What were they like? How did they get on?"

"I imagine their lives were pretty primitive, preoccupied with getting food and shelter. The land wasn't particularly good for growing crops, apart from maybe a few types of grains. Fishing was probably their main source of food. We found remnants of boats and netting fragments. Some of the villages had sheep. But here we found goat skeletons, so we know they had goats. That means goat meat, goat's milk, and probably goat skin clothing.

"What did they look like?"

"Well, physically they were probably not very different from us. The skeletons we've found are about the same size, maybe a little shorter. Their hair would have been dark and long, and the men would all have been bearded. They would have been lean and wiry, because of their diet and lifestyle."

"But then, what about my cup? Do you think somebody in this village made it?"

"Could be. We know that they learned enough metalworking to forge primitive tools—axes, knife blades, hammers, and the like. They wouldn't have been able to dig out their homes like this without digging tools. And they had metal cookware. But that thing is rather different. Usually dishes and drinking cups, if that's what it is, were made of clay. We've found plenty of shards of earthenware dishes and crockery. Metal ore was hard to find and difficult to work with, so it's puzzling why somebody would go to the trouble to make something as simple as a cup out of metal. But my colleague from Dublin will be returning with his findings in a few days, so maybe he'll be able to tell us something. "

"Maybe it meant something else? Had some other use?' Mary wondered.

"I suppose we may never know."

She could listen to Dennis talk all day. She found his genteel demeanor so much more engaging than her townsmen's bawdy joking, and his earnestness so much more impressive than her townsmen's unlearned braggadocio.

"There's something else I'm wondering about. Where did you say you found that cup?"

"Up on the ridge overlooking the sea. She pointed. "About two miles from here. Buried partway down the slope."

"That's very curious. How did it get up there? There's nothing else around. I wonder if it came from the other village."

"What other village?"

"Some colleagues have very recently found evidence of another village like this one, about six miles west of here. We call it Croaghbeg, which means 'small hill.'"

"So did the people of this other village trade with ours, or whatever?"

"They might have. But more likely they either did not know about each other, or possibly were suspicious and resentful and kept their distance. They were more likely to war with each other than trade. A village in those times was almost like a nation today, fiercely protective of its people and its identity."

"Even though they were that close?"

"They weren't that close if you had to walk it."

"So you really can't tell where the cup came from, then."

"Once again, we don't know. Maybe we should do some digging up around there, but so far, we've found nothing very far from this village. So unless somebody deliberately tossed it away up

there for some reason, you have a total mystery
here."

⊕   ⊕   ⊕   ⊕   ⊕   ⊕

*Elated, her heart light, Arlana began
virtually to skip back to her village, if that was
possible over the uneven and rocky terrain. She
made her way down the slope, weaving her way
among the rocks and boulders that studded the
terrain. She had proceeded for only a few
moments when—suddenly—a figure leaped up
from behind a boulder.*

*"Hah!" he bellowed, grabbing her hair and
yanking her to a halt.*

*Her heart pounded. She turned to look at
who it was.*

*"Father!" she cried. "What are you doing
here?"*

*"Who is he?' her father said, glaring at her
and holding his grip on her long hair.*

"There's no one."

"Do not lie to me, girl. Who is he?"

*"He is just a boy I ran into one day while
walking. We come up here from time to time and
talk."*

"Where is he from?"

"He's from Croaghbeg," she said, panting.

"And why were you with him up there?"

"I...I meet him. We talk."

"Talk!?"

"Yes! That is all. We just visit."

"You are not yet fifteen summers!"

She wriggled under his grip. "Let go of me. I have done nothing wrong."

"Nothing wrong!? What you have done is curse our tribe, that's what you have done!"

"Stop it, father! You are pulling my hair!"

"I'll do more than that if I catch you with that outlander again!"

He held her by her long tresses the entire way back to the village. When they arrived, he flung her down onto the ground in the open central area, waking many of the tribe, and announced to the village where she had been. Several of the tribesmen approached, grunting their disapproval. Some of the women clucked theirs. The priest came forward and said, "An outlander? Child, what have you done?"

"I have done nothing!" she shouted.

He commanded, "Get to bed. We will pray to the gods for forgiveness tomorrow."

Arlana protested, "But what have I done? He is just a boy, like any other. I like to talk to him. And all we did is talk."

All so far," her mother said. "Next thing that happens, I have grandchildren I will never see because they are raised over there, with his name."

"That cannot be true," Arlana said.

"Our life is here," her mother asserted. "Not in some other village."

"Our life?" Arlana replied.   "What is our life? Working every day for clothing and shelter and searching for food. If I cannot share that with someone I like, then what is the point of it all?"

"You speak heresy, child!"

Her mother shepherded Arlana into their cave dwelling. She sat her daughter down and said, "Dear, you must respect the purity of the tribe. Our tribe can only remain strong if our blood line is pure."

"Mother, I do not believe that. A person is a person, wherever they come from. There are things beyond our tribe!"

"Not for you. Now get to bed. Get some rest. Tomorrow is another long day."

She lay on her bier of pelts, tearful, despondent, turning her possible fate over and over in her mind.

Within a year she would be obligated to choose a mate. There was no one in the village she was remotely interested in. No one.

She could imagine what was going to happen. She might never be able to see Conlaoch again.   Her parents would probably rush a betrothal to insure that.

She had to risk seeing him again.   She knew what she had to ask him.

�֎   ✖   ✖   ✖   ✖   ✖

It was nearly closing time.

Mary sat at a corner table in the pub with Dennis. He had come in three hours earlier and nursed two pints waiting until she finished her duties for the evening, in order to talk to her.

"I brought your cup back," he said. He withdrew a package from his pocket and unwrapped a layer of cloth to reveal her cup, now polished and gleaming.

"Wow," she said. "They really cleaned it up."

"Yeah, it looks nice. I wanted you to see it at its best," he said.

"So, did they figure out what the symbols mean?"

"No," he replied. "They don't conform to any known runes or glyphics that we know of from the era."

"So what are they?"

"The nearest we can figure is that they have some personal meaning to the maker of the cup, perhaps a name, or else they may be purely decorative. One of the symbols looks like the moon. We can't really say. But we have the characters on file, in case we ever run into them on something else."

"Wow, so it's really one of a kind," she said, admiring it.

"There's something I wanted to ask you," he said. "Would you be willing to donate this to a museum? The British Museum might be interested."

"Really? Is it worth something?" was her reply.

"Well, I don't think anyone would want to buy it, no," he said. "I mean, it's made of common metal with no precious stones or anything else of real value. I can't imagine what an ordinary person would do with it, other than maybe to use as an ashtray. But from an archaeological point of view, it's unique. It was fashioned all those centuries ago, and we've never found anything like it, so that makes it of considerable historical interest."

She turned it over in her hands, gazing at it. "When I look at it, I can imagine some ancient craftsman, with primitive tools, laboring over it. Shaping it, carving it. I wonder, was it his first try, or maybe was he skilled and this was made for a special occasion? Too bad we can't ever know."

"You feel what we archaeologists feel when we look at an artifact," he said.

"It's like a connection to the past," she continued. "Another chapter in a continuing story. It's like with my grandfather's fiddle. Walter Sullivan takes it down from the shelf about once a month and plays it, and every time he does, I feel a connection to my grandfather. I hope my children and grandchildren get to hear that fiddle played. You say this cup is unique. Somebody made it. That person had a life in this land. They lived and died, felt joy, pain, maybe love. There's got to be a story behind this cup. I just wonder what it is."

They rose to go outside for a walk in the moonlight.

"So, don't you get tired of digging in the dirt for a living?" Mary asked.

"I get tired of the dirt, I suppose," he answered, "but I never get tired of the mystery. We know surprisingly little about the ancient peoples that lived in this country. We know some of what they left behind—their homes, their artifacts, their bones—but there's so much more we don't know. What they thought, what they felt. We don't even know what kind of language they had. Somewhere along the line Gaelic developed, but as far as the people who lived in this village, or whoever made this thing here, we don't know whether they could communicate the way we do, or with just grunts and gestures, or something in between."

"Well, I think there must have been some of them who thought about things besides food and fighting. I think they must have looked up at the sky and felt the same things we do, wondered the same things we do. What their lives meant, where they were going…."

He looked tenderly at her. "You're quite the philosophical one, aren't you?"

"When you live in a land like this, with all its ancient mysteries," she replied, "how can you not be?"

He stopped and looked into her eyes. "It is an ancient land, but it has some very lovely things today, too. Like you."

She looked up at him, the moonlight bathing his face, and gazed deep into his eyes.

He bent down and kissed her lovingly.   She yielded.

✛   ✛   ✛   ✛   ✛   ✛

The full moon once again lit Arlana's way as she trudged along the path up the hill toward their meeting spot at the top of the ridge. It had become increasingly difficult to steal away at night to meet him, but she had managed to sneak away two nights ago when the moon turned nearly full, as she always had done. And sure enough, he had been there waiting for her. Then they had made their plans.

But tonight that heavenly beacon that always guided her way had become veiled with scudding clouds. Nonetheless, she pressed on, grimly determined. By the time she reached their meeting spot overlooking the sea, the moon had become quite clouded over, and the brush and marshlands began to glisten with rain. A cold wind stirred. She tightened her pelt overwrap against the chill.

And then she saw him appear dimly in the distance. He said, as he always did, "Arlana?" And she was comforted. They rushed to each other's arms. He held her tight, not wanting to let her go.

At length, she broke from his embrace and said, "Did you bring the herbs?"

"I did," he said. He removed a wrapped satchel of coarse cloth from his tunic. He undid it to reveal a cluster of herbs and leaves.

"And this will do the trick?" she asked.

"This is what our priest uses on the animals. I have seen him do it many times. And it is enough. We only need to make a potion and heat it. I need to build a small fire."

"A fire?" she said.

"The old men of the tribe predicted rain. So I came prepared." He undid a bundle he carried on his back. Setting it on the ground, he gingerly unwrapped it to reveal kindling sticks and straw. She held her garment over him against the wind and rain as he produced flint and tinder, and in short order he had a cozy fire crackling. Then he asked her, "Did you bring it?"

From the folds of her goatskin wrap, she pulled out the metal cup and handed it over. He filled it with the collection of herbs he had brought, added water from his goatskin water bag, stirred in the herbs to make a soupy glop, and heated it through.

He grasped the cup full of steaming brew with the piece of coarse cloth and held it up to her. "Last chance. Do you still want to do this?"

"Yes. We must" she said. " I cannot go on with you, and I will not go on without you."

"Here, then."

She took it and smelled it. "It is foul."

"Of course it is foul."

Arlana allowed it to cool a moment, but was suddenly distracted by a clamor. She looked off to her right to see that a cluster of five or six men were trudging up the slope toward them, shouting and brandishing torches and spears.

"My father and men from the village!" she cried. "They found us! They must have followed me!"

They looked at each other. The shock and gravity of the moment registered in their faces.

She closed her eyes and drank some. She passed the cup to Conlaoch, and he drank.

The rain began to pour down. Thunder resounded. Lightning flashed, illuminating them for an instant.

"Arlana!" she heard her father call from down the slope.

She looked up at Conlaoch and smiled and kissed him.

"Stop them!" her father shouted from thirty yards down the hillside. The townsmen quickened their pace. "Arlana!" he shouted again, waving his torch.

Then her eyes became glassy. She began to cough and choke up. He looked at her and grimaced, his neck muscles tense, and he doubled over. They looked at each other one more time before their eyes dimmed. He collapsed upon the crest of the hill. She too fell, and then tumbled

*down the slope toward the sea several yards
before rolling to a halt. Along the way, she lost
her grip on the cup. When it landed a few feet
from where she did, the driving rain loosened a
surge of mud that rushed in and covered it
almost immediately.*

*Thunder cracked in the sky above, and the
waves roared in the sea below. Their bodies lay
there, still, until the villagers arrived to discover
to their great horror what the two young lovers
had done.*

✠   ✠   ✠   ✠   ✠   ✠

Dennis Flaherty and Mary Finnegan were
married in the village church of Cragardh on August
28, 1948. The wedding reception was held at
Finnegan's Pub, of course, with music and dancing
from early afternoon until on in to the night.

The entire town turned out in its starched
and pressed finery to wish them well. It was the
general opinion that no one had seen a grander
celebration in the town, though it must also be said
that no one could remember another day when
drinks had been free at Finnegan's Pub all day and
night.

After a sumptuous dinner of smoked ham
with whiskey sauce, garlic mashed potatoes, glazed
carrots, and salads and scones galore, the crowd fell
to the serious business of toasting the newlyweds.
One after another, the ladies and gentlemen of the
town, mostly the gentlemen, stood to raise their
glasses in one fairly long-winded tribute after

another, wishing the couple health, wealth, happiness, fertility, tranquility, and whatever else they could think of. Old Finn said what was on many a mind: "And may ye settle down here and train yer children to keep the pub running for many years to come!"

Then came the moment for Dennis to toast his bride. He stood up, and the crowd at the tables began to raise their glasses in readiness. "Just a moment," he said. "I think we need to do it this way."

From the side pocket of his white jacket he pulled out the polished metal cup of Conlaoch.

Mary, sitting next to him in her splendid white dress, said, "I thought the cup was going to the museum."

Dennis shook his head and smiled and said, "Because of this cup, I have something more precious and valuable than a museum artifact. I have you, Mary Finnegan." He turned to the crowd, raised the cup, and said, "And shouldn't it be fitting that we drink our bridal toast from the cup that brought us together?"

Amid cheers, he poured champagne into the cup, raised it to his lips and drank from it, then passed the cup to Mary, who did likewise. The crowd roared. It was the best champagne she had ever tasted.

They feasted and caroused on into the night, and from its perch behind the bar, the cup watched it all: the music, the dancing, the merriment, the stories told, the toasts raised, the old women in the corner smiling at the cavorting children, the laughter, the tears, and, at long last, the drooping eyelids and nodding heads of revelers in the wee hours finally realizing that the night must end.

The cup was never returned to any museum. Instead, regularly dusted and shined, it was ensconced in a position of honor on the shelf above the doorway between the bar and the side room, the same place where reposed Grandpa's fiddle and Grandma's tea kettle, and later Mary's father's pipe and her mother's knitting needles.

And for decades thereafter, it sat there overseeing the toasts, the music sessions, the stories, the blarney, and the daily and nightly spectacle of life that paraded before it in the pub, now run by Mary and Dennis.

Mary and Dennis had two sons, Seamus and Liam. They were both fine strapping lads with auburn hair, born eleven months apart. "Irish twins," they were called. Liam went on to study at Trinity College in Dublin and eventually got a position as a biologist in London. Seamus stayed in Cragardh and helped run the pub, eventually taking it over when it became too much for Dennis and Mary. He died in 1982, she in 1985.

In 1988, an electrical short sparked a fire that burned the pub to the ground. In the ruckus and confusion of attempting to put out the early-morning blaze, no one gave much thought to saving the cup. It was buried under charred remains and ash and dust, along with the other keepsakes and curios that had adorned the walls.

Moreover, when it came time to clear away the debris prior to rebuilding the place, it seems that the bulldozer operator had been too much in his cups the night before, so that he was none too observant when he set about clearing the ruins and scrap from the spot, paying little heed to whether he unearthed any of the antiques or other objects that had adorned the walls.

And thus the cup was buried once again in the Irish soil, and there it has lain for lo, these many years.

Afterword to "The Cup of Conlaoch"

I have long been interested in Irish music and culture. The Milwaukee area where I live boasts a huge Celtic culture, with Irish pubs, parades, cultural centers, and the largest Irish summer music festival in North America, Irish Fest.

I have also been to Ireland, where I learned that one cannot visit without becoming immersed in a sense of history. Its past is displayed or suggested everywhere. Long- abandoned castle ruins dot the landscape. Every pub seems to have old artifacts lining its walls. In Ireland, I saw the ruins of an ancient village being slowly excavated and researched, and realized how much of Ireland's history must be layered beneath the soil. What stories might lie behind all the stone walls and buried artifacts? What stories could all those museum objects tell?

So I tried to spin an Irish tale, linking modern day with the past. Slàinte.

In the Coffee Shop

It was crowded in the coffee shop, but I had time to wait. I stood in line, zoning out on the dark green and caramel colors of the décor and the servers' aprons. It smelled good—the robust aroma of freshly-ground beans wafted throughout, punctuated with notes of cinnamon and chocolate. Hmmm, chocolate. Though I had planned on just a regular to go, I changed my mind and decided to go for a large mocha. Whipped cream, sir? Sure, what the heck.

I took my white mug over to a table, sat down, and began to peruse the paper. Then I heard, "Scott?" I turned to look.

She was sipping from a big mug of chai at the next table.

"Beth?"

"Actually, it's Liz now."

"Really?"

"Yeah. My kids liked Liz."

"Kids?"

"Two daughters. One's in junior high, and one just got married last year."

"Wow. That's great. And your husband is....?"

"Bill. He's an engineer."

"Bill." Hmm. Was that the one she vaguely referred to when we broke up, or were there others in between?

"We're split up," she supplied. "Long story. But how are you?"

"I lost my wife two years ago."

"Oh. Sorry."

"Thanks," I said, and then quickly moved onto "Gee, how long has it been?" trying to be nonchalant. I knew exactly how long. Thirty-two years, two months. Fifteen months before the date of my wedding.

Her hairdo had changed—it was now straight, swooping down on sides, slightly turned under at the ends. Very stylish. Brown, with blond highlights. But were those gray roots underneath? I didn't ask. It didn't matter.

"So, do you still play guitar?"

She chuckled. "It's sitting in the closet gathering dust. You know how it is—kids, home repairs, chores. Life gets away from you."

I could see her sitting cross-legged in front of the campfire, strumming her guitar. I listened to her in front of the crackling logs, song after song. I knew nothing about guitar, but I liked her choice of songs and her singing voice. I remember wondering whether maybe she had a career in music ahead of her.

That was our very special camping weekend. The weekend we first made love.

Trying to think of another music-related question, the only thing I could come up with was, "So are Seals and Crofts on your iPod?"

She furrowed her brow for an instant at the question, and then she smiled and said, "Oh, yeah. They are. Haven't listened to them in quite a while, though."

It was a week before Christmas, and I stopped to give her the album before heading out of town to visit my family. It was snowing, and snowflakes fell on the wrapping as I handed it to her. She giggled as she opened the wrapping and saw the album cover.

She had been hinting for some time about how she liked them and would like their greatest hits album, but she was working in a low-paying job and living with her parents and didn't really want to splurge for albums.

Did she remember? I was reading so much into her pauses, her brows, her expression.

I asked her about what she was doing now. She started to tell me about her job, but I confess to fogging out after a bit. I became entranced in watching her eyes—still that scintillating green-blue—and her lips as she spoke—still puckishly rounded, soft, expressive—that I almost lost her thread.

"I like looking at faces," she had told me on the night we met. "Everybody says it's the eyes, but I find so much in the mouth, the lips, the expression."

The rest of the time, I watched her lips as she spoke, their curves, their subtle movements, and especially the smiles.

Before that night was out, I was kissing those lips. It was exciting.

I had never done that before, after just meeting someone. Later, she told me that neither had she. The spark was just there.

Back to reality. "I didn't know you lived around here," I said.

"I live in Fairvale, about a half hour away. I'm running errands and just stopped in. I'm surprised I haven't seen you here more often."

"Yeah, what a fluke."

"Do you still sing in the Community Chorus?"

"Yes, I have been. You remember that?"

Do I remember?   I can't forget sitting on that hard metal chair, watching her standing in the third row of the community chorus concert that year, seeing the joy and expressiveness on her face as she sang out.   I guess that was the moment I decided I loved her.

"What happened to…that guy?" I hesitated, not remembering his name, the one she broke it off for. "The ranch guy."

"Oh. That ended.   I came back a little sorer and a little wiser," was all she would allow.

It was the evening of that last, awkward date.   I had gotten tickets a month earlier for this play, but during that month a lot had happened with us.   She told me on the thirty-five-minute drive back from the theater.   She had casually mentioned two weeks before that she had met some other "interesting" guy at a party.   And then she dropped the bombshell: "He asked me to come out to this ranch he's working on for the summer, and I'm going to go."

I knew why.   The relationship had grown stale.   She wanted something new.   She had even mentioned a few weeks before about how she had been feeling "cool" toward me.

On her doorstep, I hesitated, and she said, "You can kiss me if you want."   As if we were starting out, instead of ending.   But ending we were—with no argument, no bang, not even a whimper. It just ended.

I'd love to know what happened, but this wasn't the time to get into that. She wasn't going to tell me everything she'd been doing for thirty years, though I would have listened. I couldn't stop gazing at her face.

The years had been kind. The lines on her face were soft, not etched, especially the subtle laugh lines around her eyes. It had probably been a good life.

She broke that train of thought by rising and saying, "Well, I gotta go. I have an appointment. It was good to see you, Scott."

"Yeah, you too. Really nice."

She began to get up, and then stopped and reached into her bag for a piece of paper and a pen. She scribbled down a number and passed it over.

I looked at the paper and hesitated, wondering, "You're giving me your number?"

"Maybe you might want to give me a call some time," she said.

"Really?" was all I could manage to respond with.

"Sure. For old times' sake."

I watched her walk out the door, and I flashed on the dozen things I had on my mind—appointments, groceries, oil change, haircut….

I stared at the paper. I finished my mocha. I crumpled up the paper and rose to leave. Halfway out the door, I stopped. I turned around and walked back to the table.

I picked up the crumpled paper and stuck it in my pocket and turned to walk out the door.

Afterword to "In the Coffee Shop"

I have always been intrigued by the question "What might have happened if...?" Particularly when it comes to relationships. Do people still think about their first or early loves, long gone from their lives? What happens if they meet again by chance? Can we ever go back?

This is a short short story, which I am told is something of a trend in fiction today. Publishers think that the public is impatient with long works and prefers quick reads that can be digested on a subway ride or during a lunch hour. (I'm not sure about that—George R. R. Martin, Diana Gabaldon, and Stephen King seem to be doing all right with their 900-page behemoths.)

Anyway, I thought I'd try my hand at a quickie. It's challenging to figure out what to do in under 1500 words (some sources say under 1000). You can't really have proper plot development and resolution. So I chose to go with a vignette, just a scene, a suggestion of what was and what might be. If you want the full story, you'll have to fill in the details yourself.

The Highwayman

(with apologies to Alfred Noyes and Phil Ochs)

The wind howled through the trees and across the moors, and clouds scudded across the night sky like wispy seas bearing up the ghostly galleon that was the waxing moon.

A lone rider galloped along the solitary road, pale white in the moonlight, that cut through the darkly shadowed heath.

The glowing warmth of an inn beckoned in the distance. The rider galloped up and reined in his chestnut roan, its hooves clattering on the cobblestones in the entrance yard before the two-story lath and plaster structure. Above him, the sign reading "Bull and Feathers Inn" in faded lettering swung creakily back and forth.

Tim, the hostler, ran forth from the stables to tend to the visitor's mount, the wind reddening his boyish face and rustling his mousy hair. After turning over the reins of his horse, the visitor pulled the cast iron latch on the worn oaken door and entered.

Inside, he was pleased to find warmth and laughter. A large fire roared and crackled in the massive stone fireplace on one side, and at least a dozen patrons sat at the rough-hewn oaken tables carousing and telling tales. The aromas of savory stew, wood smoke, and pipe tobacco wafted throughout.

A comely serving girl breezed at his table and cheerily asked, "And how are you this fine evenin'?"

"Evening I'll grant you, but fine is debatable," said the stranger.

"Aye, 'tis cold indeed out there," she replied with a pleasant smile. "Are you hungry, then?"

"What's good tonight?"

"Well, we have our cheeses and meat pies. But how about some stew to warm ye?"

"That sounds fine."

"It'll be a minute. Pint of ale while you're waitin', sir?"

"Love one."

She brought him a tankard of ale. His first sip was hearty and satisfying. He looked around at the cheery atmosphere of the place. One of the patrons played a tin whistle at a corner table, with his three tablemates clapping in time. The stranger smiled. It had been some time since he had felt particularly merry.

He watched the young woman carry on with her duties, cheerfully serving the food and drink, clearing plates and mugs, joking with the regulars. He observed the way her pleasing form moved gracefully beneath her long gingham skirt and apron. Her raven-black hair hung in graceful strands around her shoulders, and her dark eyes and fair skin were fetching to the eye. Her charm and quick wit brightened the gloom of the evening.

In due course she delivered his stew, setting down the bowl and accompanying pewter plate with crusty bread and dollop of butter. "Here you go, sir." As he picked up the knife, she added, "You're new around here, aren't you?"

Smiling at the opportunity to chat with her, he replied, "No, but I haven't been in these parts for some time."

"What name do ye go by, then?"

"I'm William Blackfriar."

"Well, Mr. Blackfriar, I'm Bess." She pointed to the portly, red-faced bartender with stringy gray hair. "And that'll be my father, Albert, who owns the place. He—"

Her attention was suddenly turned toward the entrance. A group of three red-coated soldiers, a lieutenant and two privates, entered the inn, loud and boisterous. Joking and jostling each other, they commandeered a table near the fire. "Oh, Lord," she whispered. "It was a nice night until they showed up."

"Serving wench!" one of them called. "Drinks!"

She strode dutifully over to their table, whereupon they ordered, loudly, "Ale all around!"

As she turned to walk away toward the bar, they ogled her, making sniggering comments. When she returned and bent to serve the trayful of brimming tankards, one of the soldiers slapped her behind and bellowed, "That's me gal!" The others brayed with laughter.

"Please, sir!" She tried, awkwardly, to laugh it off.

The lieutenant wrapped his arm around her waist and yanked her toward him. "C'mere, love. It's cold outside. How about a little warmth?"

She resisted. He grasped her more tightly.

"Please, sir, I beg of you!"

"Oh, come on now, love. Give us a kiss. There'll be a tip in it for ye!"

Irritated, Bess tried to break free of his grip, crying, "Let me go!"

The lieutenant persisted. She dropped her empty tray and struck him on the arm, but he only tightened his grip on her waist.

William Blackfriar arose and walked over to the soldiers.

He clasped the lieutenant on the shoulder from behind and said, in a low, firm tone, "Leave her alone."

The lieutenant turned and said, "Well, what do we have here?" He looked up and down at

Blackfriar, his leer turning easily to a smirk, and said, "Back off."

"I said leave her alone."

The lieutenant released the girl, drink still dabbling his lips, and stood to face Blackfriar. Though he was shorter than Blackfriar, the sandy-haired, wiry officer rose to his full height, his countenance stern and his eyes beetling. "I'll thank you to mind your own business," he sneered. The music and laughter ceased.

"And I'll thank you to leave the lady alone," Blackfriar replied softly, "or I'll make it my business."

"All right, then," said the lieutenant, his manner becoming unctuous. He turned away as if to sit back down, but then whirled and cocked his fist back to strike. But before he could, Blackfriar slammed a right fist into his face, knocking him backward and bloodying his nose.

From Blackfriar's right, the nearer private moved to grab him, but with almost a single movement, Blackfriar flung his fist back and slammed it backhanded into the private's face. The private reeled backward.

The other private, to his left, drew a pistol from his belt. Blackfriar swung a hard backhanded left to knock the gun arm aside, then turned to seize the gunman's forearm and wrest the weapon from him. It dropped to the floor. The private then tried to take a swing, but Blackfriar blocked it and kneed him in the midriff to send him reeling as well.

The bloodied lieutenant recovered enough to lunge at Blackfriar, but Blackfriar drove a hard fist into his stomach and then delivered a solid uppercut. The lieutenant sank to his knees, and the two privates held off any further efforts.

They had had quite enough, even before the innkeeper came out from behind the bar, shouting, "All right, that's it!" Cursing and waving his arms, Albert berated the three soldiers, "I've had more than enough of the likes of you! Out! Now!"

The lieutenant rose to his full height, managing a swagger even as his nose bled, and said unctuously, "I'll leave only to avoid making a mess of the place and spoiling the evening. But you"— he turned to face Blackfriar—"if I were you, I'd not cross my path again."

Grumbling and glaring at their assailant, the soldiers shuffled out the door into the night.

The innkeeper then turned to Blackfriar and said, "Sir, as you stood up for my daughter's honor, I'd be proud to have you remain. Enjoy your supper, and there'll be no charge for it, either."

The other patrons settled back in to the low buzz of friendly conversation, and Blackfriar returned to his table.

When she had a moment, the serving girl came and sat down on a bench opposite him. She smiled, her dark eyes glistening from the firelight, and said warmly, "Thank you, Mister...Blackfriar, is it?"

"Not exactly your favorite customers, I'm guessing."

She shook her black locks. "That lieutenant—Stewart's his name —he's a hothead. Loves a quarrel."

"I can tell."

"But you'd best be careful messing about with the likes of him. He's not somebody you'd want to be on the wrong side of."

"I'll keep that in mind."

Bess took note of a pause in the atmosphere of the inn, a lull wherein she did not have anything to tend to for the moment, so that she could indulge her desire to chat further with Blackfriar. He took note of that, as well, as she sat at his table.

"Is the supper all right, then?"

"It's delicious," he said, taking a bite of the bread.

"So what brings you here? Passing through?"

"I'm on my way home, to see my father."

"So you've been away, have you?"

"I've been in the army. Yes, the same King's army that lot belongs to, though I've been stationed far from here." He took a draught from his tankard and continued, "It's been years since I've seen him. He wrote a few times, but I've been transferred so many places, including at sea for a while, that the mail couldn't keep up with me. I received a few letters of his long after they were sent, and in them he referred to others I'd never gotten. I'm quite out of touch with my family. It isn't even my family any more—just my aging father. Everyone else is gone. So my term is up and I've come back to see how he's managing the family manor."

"Where is it?"

"In the next county. I don't think I'll make it there tonight. Have you got a room?"

She smiled. "We do, indeed. I'll have Father fix you up."

Though she needed to return to her duties, she smiled and glanced toward him each time she passed his table. He was tall, and she could tell he was possessed of a solid build, even beneath his loose tunic with ruffled sleeves. Under his tousled brown hair and stubbly beard, she took note of his handsome features, his strong chin, and his dark brown eyes. She was pleased that he would be staying the night.

After his supper, she led him up the creaky stairs to a room on the second floor. The accommodations were modest, quite rustic, but all he wanted was a place to sleep. She produced a folded wool blanket from a closet and handed it to him, saying, "You might want this. It'll be cold tonight." As he took it from her, she let her hand brush against his as she looked him in the eye. He noted that her touch lingered just a trice longer than it needed to. "And thank you again for sticking up for me," she added. "Most of our customers would just sit back and laugh at the show."

"I couldn't imagine doing that," he smiled, looking into her glistening dark eyes. "Good night."

He arose early the next morning and enjoyed a modest but satisfying breakfast of biscuits, sausages, and tea. He managed to smile once or twice at Bess, though she was bustling around with early-morning tasks.

As he saddled his horse in the stable yard and prepared to leave, he saw Bess approach. She said, "Here. Take this." She handed him a parcel wrapped in cloth and bound with string.

"What is it?"

"A meat pie and some cheese. You might need it. There's no other inn where you're headed."

"Thank you. How much will that be?"

"Just take it."

He tucked it into his saddle bag. Then he smiled, clasping his hand gently on her shoulder, taking one last look into her ebon eyes, and turned to mount and spurred off. Down the road a few yards, he looked back and waved. She waved back.

He cantered all morning at a leisurely pace, stopping at a glade about midday to enjoy his meat pie and some of the cheese. At length, the wooded countryside became more familiar as he neared the manor of his boyhood home. He came across a large, stately oak, onto whose gnarled trunk he found a notice nailed. In crude type, it read:

Auction.
Blackfriar Estate.

Noon, September 14 and 15.

Auction? he wondered. *Why would there be an auction?*

He arrived in the early afternoon. A huge crowd had gathered in front of the country estate in which he had spent his boyhood, a two-story stucco house which now seemed dilapidated and in disrepair. Furniture and other items were being carried out the main entrance near an auctioneer's platform in the front yard.

Blackfriar approached the makeshift table that had been set up along the sidelines near the auction platform and said, "What's going on here?"

The thin, owly, bespectacled man behind the table looked up from his documents and said, "Seems plain enough. We're auctioning off the place."

"But why?"

"Debts. At least half the proceeds will go to pay off his debts. And as for the rest, such as it is, there's no family to pass it onto. So it becomes the property of the crown, to dispense with."

"But I'm William! I'm Arthur Blackfriar's son!"

"Are you, now? Well, sir, it seems that Arthur died last month."

"What?" Blackfriar was taken aback. "My father's dead?"

"Fell from his horse," the harried clerk said, about as matter-of-factly as he could. "And he left no will, naming you nor anybody else."

"He didn't think he needed to. I was his only family. This place should be mine!"

"It's not that simple, sir. You needed to file a declaration. You never signed the paper."

Blackfriar shook his head. "I was away in the army. I was in Northern Ireland, and then I was in France. Serving the King."

"No matter, sir. We tried to locate you. We sent you a letter about his death, and then we sent a notice with the papers to sign."

"I never got those letters."

"I'm sorry, sir. Nothin' I can do. The place is sold. What's done is done. All that's left is this auction of the furnishing and miscellaneous belongings."

Blackfriar's brow furrowed and his jaw tightened. "So you're telling me I have no recourse, no claim to anything on the place?"

"If you want something, you can bid on it, like anyone else."

Blackfriar said through gritted teeth, "This is not over!" and walked away.

He stood at the edge of the crowd for a few moments and watched the auction bidding. He saw that they were selling some furniture. He recognized tables, chairs, and a settee that had been in his home for years. He wished he could buy some of the furniture, but he had only his horse to transport it and no place to take it. Gradually, the realization sank in that he was homeless.

The auction progressed to smaller items. The auctioneer held up and opened a small wooden box which Blackfriar recognized. "What am I bid for this handsome pistol?" the auctioneer sang out.

"One shilling," someone called.

"One shilling, tuppence," Blackfriar said.

"One shilling, four," someone else called.

"One shilling, sixpence!" he heard himself shout.

He got it for two shillings, a greater sum than he had wanted to pay and one that left a considerable dent in his cash purse. But he now owned something of his father's estate.

When he went to the clerk's desk to pay for the item, he asked, "What is to be done with the proceeds from the sale?"

"Why, it goes to His Majesty, of course. It'll be sent to London tomorrow, after we finish."

Twilight approached, and as he watched the crowd disperse and the auctioneers pack up for the day, he wondered what to do for the night. He noticed that no one seemed to be paying attention to the barns. He led his mount over to the most distant one, a smaller barn where horses had been kept, pushed open the large door, and entered. As he suspected, the barn was deserted. The horses had long since been removed.

He led his horse down the center row between the stalls until he came to one that had an accumulation of dry straw still in the mow. His famished steed eagerly took to the pile. "I'll get you some water in a moment," Blackfriar said, patting the animal's mane.

While his horse grazed, Blackfriar opened
up the wooden box and took out his father's pistol.
He held it up to the faint sunlight streaming in from
the gaps in the barn wall boards. He cocked the
hammer and checked the trigger.   It was not a
particularly fancy weapon, and it would have to be
cleaned, but it appeared serviceable.   He then
rummaged through the box to find a small satchel of
leaden pistol balls, some wadding pads, and a
powder flask about half full.

"Well, let's see if you work, then."   He
loaded the pistol with powder and tamped a ball and
wadding down the barrel with the ramrod.   He
looked around for a suitable target, settling on the
rusty carcass of an oil lamp hanging near the
doorway perhaps two dozen paces away. He held
the pistol at arm's length to sight it, cocked the
hammer, and fired. The ball pinged off the metal of
the lamp as the blast echoed and the acrid haze of
smoke hung in the air.   His horse reared and
whinnied at the noise.

"You might have to get used to that, my
friend," Blackfriar said, pleased that the pistol
worked.

He reloaded the pistol and tucked it and its
accessories into his saddle bag, near where his
service saber from the army was sheathed. Now he
had a saber and a pistol. But what could he do with
those?

Glancing around the barn, Blackfriar was
moved to recall the times he had spent here as a

boy. His memory then flashed upon something his father always kept here. Might it still be here? He walked down to the last stall and looked at the wall next to the gate. Sure enough, there it was. Hanging on a peg nearly out of sight on the wall was his father's coat, the one he had always kept in the barn in case he worked late and it got chilly, to save him the trouble of going up to the house. No one had bothered to take it.

He picked it up, shook it out, and looked it over. It was in passable condition, not moth-eaten and not too dirty. He tried it on and found that it fit. It was a long brown coat, coming down nearly to his knees, and complete with a hood to protect against the wind and rain. Perhaps he could use it.

He unsaddled and tended to his horse, then plumped up a comfortable pile of straw to rest upon. Donning the coat for warmth, and tucking his pistol and saber next to him, he settled in for the night.

He lay there gazing at the slivers of moonlight filtering through the weathered rafters. His thoughts turned to the uncertainty of what to do next. He had no home to go back to. He had no personal fortune and no place to turn.

He wasted no time feeling sorry for himself. He had never been one for self-pity. Instead, his uncertainty, his incredulity over his situation progressed quickly to anger. He began to seethe with rage at the turn of events today until he drifted off to sleep.

The next morning, the crowd of buyers, sellers and onlookers again gathered in the yard to conclude the auction. The remaining furnishings, paintings, implements, and kitchen supplies were sold off.

Blackfriar loitered near the outskirts of the crowd. He did not even want to enter the house and look around. He watched in mute anger as the last of the sold household goods were loaded up onto various carriages and wagons to be carted off.

Torn between galloping off in disgust and remaining to glean more information, he decided to once again approach the officious little sales agent, now harried and busy tallying up the final receipts. A single redcoat soldier with musket at the ready stood guard next to the table.

"Excuse me," he said politely. "Is the sale complete?"

"Yeah, obviously," said the gaunt agent, without looking up from his ledger. "Didn't bring in too much, I must say."

"How is the money being sent to London?"

"Why, by courier and coach, of course. That coach right there." He indicated a handsome stagecoach hitched to four steeds that waited nearby.

"Will it be safe?"

"Of course. A king's soldier, like this one"—he pointed to the guard—"will be along."

Blackfriar moved on. He walked to the distant barn, saddled his horse, and rode off, heading for the woods away from the main entrance lane and out of sight of the remaining crowd.

He rode for many miles, turning over in his mind what to do. He did not know where to head. He just rode aimlessly on, bitter resentment festering in his heart. He began to ponder—a coach plying the winding roads to London through woodland and heath…a satchelful of money that rightfully belonged to him…one guard….

He determined that he could not simply ride away. He must do something. And suddenly, almost instinctively, he made his decision.

The stagecoach bearing the proceeds from the auction rolled along the rutted road that wended its way through the heath, its four horses cantering at a steady, leisurely pace. The red-coated soldier sitting next to the driver nearly dozed in the afternoon sun.

Suddenly, from up ahead, they heard "Halt!"

The driver looked to see a mounted man standing in the middle of the road. He was dressed in a long, brown coat with a hood pulled over his head, and his face was covered with a scarf. He held a pistol on them.

"Stop, I say!" he shouted again.

"Drive on past him," the guard said. "He'll get out of the way soon enough."

"What, and risk getting shot?" the driver replied. "That's what you're here for, Private."

The coachman tugged on the reins until the horses slowed to a stop a few yards in front of the mounted man. As they halted, the redcoat guard reached into his belt for his pistol. The mounted man fired his. The guard cried out and seized his forearm in pain, dropping the pistol to the ground. With one swift move, the horseman tucked his now-empty pistol away and drew a saber.

Brandishing his weapon, he commanded, "Get down, all of you. Now!"

Three passengers emerged from the interior of the coach, two well-dressed women and an older man, smartly appointed. The horseman dismounted and dashed to seize the dropped pistol from the ground before the soldier and the driver climbed down and joined them on the roadway next to the coach.

"Now, let's have the money," he said, leveling the pistol at them.

"What money?" said the driver.

"You know very well what money. Let's have it. Or I'll run you through."

"It's up there," the driver pointed. "In the front boot."

The masked man stepped onto the front wheel hub and climbed briskly up to the driver's seat and reached down into the front boot to retrieve a canvas satchel. He opened it to confirm its contents, then scrambled down, continuing to hold the group at bay with the second pistol.

One of the women said, "I suppose you'll be wanting my jewels, you blackguard!"

"No. Just this." The woman arched her eyebrows in muted surprise.

"You'll never get away with this!" said the redcoat soldier, still rubbing his bleeding arm.

"I already have!" the masked man said triumphantly, thrusting the satchel into his saddle bag. He mounted his horse and turned to gallop off down the road.

Several hours later, well after dark, William Blackfriar reined in his horse in the yard of the Bull and Feathers Inn. He tethered his mount apart from the main stable. He did not really want Tim the stable-boy to scrutinize the animal too closely or become curious about the contents of his saddlebag.

Quietly he scaled the rear stairs to enter the second floor, where he found Bess tending to her room-cleaning chores. He stood in the shadows of the doorway for a moment, silently, watching her. He then said softly, "Hello, Bess."

"Mr. Blackfriar!" she said, startled, looking up.

He smiled. "Will."

"You're back," she said, alternately surprised and pleased to see him. "Weren't you going to live at your father's place?"

"Well, plans have changed a bit. The house is sold, auctioned off. It's not mine."

"How unfortunate.   Have you come back here to stay the night, then?"

"I can't stay the night. I just came by to see you. And maybe," he added with a grin, "to pick up one of your meat pies."

"To see me?"

"I just wanted to say something to you. I'll have to leave here soon. But I feel alone, and I don't want to be. How would you like to come away with me?"

"What?"

"I can't remain around here. I'm going to have to go away. I want someone to go with me."

"But go where?"

"Wherever you like.   Perhaps to France. Perhaps to America."

She was taken aback at the boldness of the idea.   "But...but how could you?" she sputtered. "How would you live?"

"I've got money now. Almost enough. I can get more."

"You do? You can?"

"I can get all we need. All we have to do is get away from here. What do you say? Did you want to spend the rest of your life tending this inn?"

"But I can't leave my father!"

"How about if I leave him enough money to take care of him in his old age? He can sell this place and move to a nice town house."

"You've got enough money for that? How is it then that I keep seeing you in the same set o' clothes each time?"

"That'll change. If you want to say no, say no. But if you say yes, mean it."

She gazed into his eyes, plumbing their depths, seeking confirmation of his sincerity. She had to admit that she was stirred by the idea. "I...I don't know," she said. "This is so sudden."

"Do me the favor of thinking about it. I'll be back. I don't know exactly when, but soon."

She fetched him a meat pie and some bread, for which he paid more than she asked. Tucking it under his arm for a moment, he seized her by the shoulders and kissed her hard and quick on the lips. Then he turned to leave, hurrying down the rear stairs.

She felt light-headed. As she looked through the window to watch him rear his steed up on its hind legs, and then turn to gallop off, she felt her heart palpitate.

She was not the only one to watch him gallop away. Young Tim also took note of Blackfriar's departure, as he had taken note of most of their conversation he could hear from his stable post. He found what he heard most troubling. For Tim had for some time nurtured in his bosom a longing for the landlord's daughter Bess. Though he knew that he was aught but a slow-witted stable boy and her love was something he could never hope to win, yet it was a yearning he was powerless to repress. The scruffy young lad with the pockmarked skin and ragged clothing had never been able to muster the courage or find the words to declare his feelings. He had feared that she would scoff at him and make him feel all the worse.

But now this vagabond had come in and, in the space of a few days, swept her off her feet. His heart ached—and his jaw clenched—as he watched the stranger ride away.

William Blackfriar waylaid a second coach the following night, this time an unguarded coach on the road to Dover. He relieved the passengers of their purses, gold, and silver and sent them on their way.

As he galloped off into the moor, he realized that he was too far from the inn and closer to his father's lands. Guided by the moonlight in a nearly cloudless sky, he chose to return to the humble straw of the abandoned barn and bed down, confident that he could hide there safely until morning.

Twittering birds accompanied the rising sun casting its pale light through the trees and across the fields. The early-morning haze had just begun to lift when, some fifty yards from the old barn, five horses bearing red-coated soldiers came to a stop in the dewy fields.

Lieutenant Stewart sat tall in his saddle, his military bearing only somewhat undermined by the purplish bruise on his nose, which gave his normally sneering baritone a bit of nasal twang.

"Sergeant?"

"Sah!"

"Light the torches."

"Yes, sah." The sergeant and three of the privates produced whittled tree limbs whose ends had been steeped in pitch. One private struck a flint to kindle a spark, and in a moment, orange flames flared and licked one and then all four torches. The four soldiers galloped toward the barn, and when they got near enough, flung their torches toward it. Three landed on the roof; one crashed through a window.

The crackling flames spread and soon began to engulf the old, weathered wood. Smoke poured out of the windows. Lieutenant Stewart watched intently from his mount, waiting. Tense moments passed.

Then they saw a door on one end of the barn fling open, and out galloped William Blackfriar, his head down and his horse's hooves thundering.

"Get him!" shouted Stewart.

The five soldiers gave chase. Blackfriar headed across the fields and toward the trees in the distance. One private fired his musket, but the ball whizzed above Blackfriar's head, the inaccuracy the result of the jostling from the private's galloping mount. Another private, spurring his steed, charged in toward Blackfriar, nearly catching up to him, and raised his pistol. Blackfriar drew his own pistol and fired back at him, knocking the soldier from the saddle.

Blackfriar veered to the left and headed for the trees bordering the farm. The sergeant fired his pistol, but from too far away to be accurate.

A fourth charged into the woods diagonally, attempting to head Blackfriar off, and then spurred his mount to gain on Blackfriar from the right. The private had no firearm, but drew his sword. Blackfriar drew his saber and brandished it high.

As the private neared him, he swung his blade at Blackfriar. Blackfriar ducked the blow. The soldier swung again, and Blackfriar blocked him. Their blades clashed and clanged as they flailed at each other in mid-gallop.

Blackfriar veered his mount to the left, to avoid the slashing blade. The soldier spurred his horse to charge in closer. Blackfriar swiped his saber, slicing the private in the arm. The private lunged at Blackfriar, but Blackfriar lashed out again, cutting a gash in the private's cheek. The private pulled back, in pain, and Blackfriar galloped ahead.

The first private, in an attempt to atone for missing his shot, raked his spurs mercilessly into the side of his mount until he had nearly caught up to his quarry.

Blackfriar, his saber still in his hand, swiped it backhanded against the soldier's jaw. The soldier recoiled and tried to leap from his mount onto Blackfriar's horse. Blackfriar swung the sword back again, but this time with a downward stroke, catching the soldier in the torso in mid-leap and causing him to tumble onto the ground, howling in pain.

Blackfriar galloped ahead, swerving around trees, leaping over fallen trunks, and disappearing into the distance.

"Let him go!" Stewart shouted as he reined in his mount, realizing the futility of pursuing the fugitive any farther through the thickening woods.

He surveyed the damage—one man shot and possibly dead, two more cut down and bleeding on the ground.

"We need to get more men," he muttered.

The Bull and Feathers Inn had begun to settle down for the night. The fire in the great stone fireplace had ebbed to glowing embers, and a few patrons lingered over their ale and pipes. Albert had put away the last of the clean tankards and cups and had begun to wipe down the bar when the oaken door slammed open. In stomped Lieutenant Stewart and four soldiers.

"We're closin', gentlemen," Albert said, "unless you want a room."

While the soldiers fanned out and stood with hands upon their swords or pistols in their belts, Stewart strode over to the bar and said officiously, "What I want is the highwayman. Is he here?"

"Highwayman?"

"Yes." Stewart stood straight up to his full height of five feet ten, his chin extended. He pulled off his gloves, finger by finger. "A wanted criminal. An outlaw who's been holding up coaches in the area. I have reason to believe he might have come here."

"Sorry, lieutenant, I'm 'fraid he's not here," Albert said, returning to his tasks. "All you'll find here are payin' guests, and there's not a thief among 'em, far as I can tell."

"Then if you've nothing to hide," Stewart said resolutely, "you won't mind if we look around."

"Don't be disturbin' my guests!" Albert called, but Stewart and his men had already begun to pound up the stairs. At the top of the creaking staircase, they found Bess tending to the linens.

Stewart said, "Well, if it isn't the lovely Bess."

"What are you doin' here, lieutenant?"

"We're looking for an outlaw, a brigand who's been robbing coaches. We think he might be here."

"There's no brigand here. There's nothin' here you want."

"Are you quite certain?" he smirked, eyeing her figure, up and down, beneath her peasant bodice and work skirt.

Bess furrowed her brow. "It's late, lieutenant. We're closin' for the night. We have two payin' guests in their rooms who'd like to get some sleep about now. We don't harbor outlaws."

He stared into her dark eyes. "You realize that if you lie to me, or deceive me, you are deceiving your King. And that's treasonous." She averted her gaze.

"I'm an honest innkeeper, and I'll thank you not to call me treasonous!" they heard Albert declare as he plodded up the stairs. When he reached the top, a bit red-faced, he continued, "There's no highwayman here, and if there was, I think we'd know."

Stewart sidled up to the innkeeper's face and oozed, "I certainly hope not, for your sake, and the sake of your daughter. You have a nice place here, innkeeper. Your ale is good, and your food is savory. If you swear that you are harboring no outlaw, I will take your word for it without tearing the place apart. But I would hate to see this charming place closed down because the pair of you are in prison for aiding and abetting."

Albert scowled. "Get out, unless you're prepared to put money on the bar!" Stewart turned and led his men tramping down the stairs, Albert following them.

Bess pretended to return to her linens, but listened carefully until she was certain that her father was occupied downstairs and she could see from the hallway window that the soldiers had galloped away. Then she reached with a broom handle to rap upon the attic door three feet above her head. It opened, and through the doorway appeared first the dusty boots, then the legs and torso of William Blackfriar, who dropped lightly to the floor.

He grasped her shoulders and said, "Thank you."

"That was close," she said. "What you're doing is dangerous, Will. I'm frightened."

He encircled her in his strong arms. "Don't be. I just need to get a little more and then it'll be over. And that Stewart is a swaggering fool."

"No, he's not. He's ruthless and determined."

"Well, he's gone now."

"Yes, but I don't like deceiving my father. You heard what the lieutenant said."

"All right. Just let me stay here tonight. I'll leave in the morning. Do you have an empty bed?"

She smiled coyly, her eyes softening. "Is that what you want—an empty bed?"

She led him into one of the bedrooms. He closed the door.

She stood gazing at him, a bit nervous, her heart pounding. He encircled her in his arms and they kissed, passionately, feverishly.

Almost as one movement, they sat upon the bed. He ran his fingers up and down her back. She breathed deeply, trembling. The strings of her bodice ripped apart under his fingers.

$\mathcal{A}$ chilly mist rolled across the moor, obscuring the early morning sun and drenching the distant road in dewy, swirling haze.

From out of the mist, Will Blackfriar reared his horse to a halt to read a poster nailed to a great oak:

Notice

£ 100 Reward!
For information leading
To the Capture of
The Highwayman
Currently terrorizing the
Countryside

He tore the poster off the tree and rode on, grimly determined.

Blackfriar had become a bitter man. He was distraught at the loss of his father. He was vexed that he had served the Crown only to find that his service was the reason he had lost his home and his fortune. He was galled by pompous, self-serving snakes like Stewart who abused the authority of the uniform.

He was also surprised at how easy it had been to hold up coaches. Passengers and drivers cowered in fear and wanted no trouble. His only regret was that one or two hauls had not provided enough to support his plans.

The path he had taken was not without its risks. He had become a wanted man. He could not find honest employment now. He had no place to stay. He could not return to the abandoned estate of his father. Nor could he stay every night at the Bull and Feathers, though that was his desire. He had been compelled to spend a few nights in the forest, but he told Bess he would return. All he needed was one more run.

Bess was his shining light in the darkness. When he was with her, it was all worthwhile. She gave him purpose. It was for her that he ran the risk of going to a village in the next county to buy some new breeches, a shirt with ruffled lace trim at the collar, a burgundy-red velvet doublet, and a tri-cornered hat. And he had gotten a shave. He imagined her smile when she saw him. Indeed, he would have stayed longer and spent more of his booty on something for her, but he spotted a group of redcoat soldiers coming out of the local tavern and decided to hastily slip away.

Blackfriar heard the coach from Waybury in the distance. Nearly on time, he noted as he replaced his pocket watch in his new doublet and adjusted the scarf over his face. And no guard next to the driver—even better. Drawing one of his pistols, he waited until the team clopped a little closer, then trotted out from the glade that concealed him and shouted, "Hold! Stand and deliver!"

The driver promptly reined in the horses as the highwayman stood in the middle of the roadway. One of the four passengers inside the coach was a young woman, who looked out the window at the dashing horseman and whispered, "Oh, my."

A white-haired gentleman in silken waistcoat and frock next to her said, "Don't be charmed by romantic notions, Miss. He's a desperate criminal and he'll shoot you down as soon as look at you. You'd best give him your valuables and hope he goes on his way without hurting anyone."

The man sitting opposite her, dressed in a nondescript dark cloth coat and breeches, said, "If I have anything to say about it, he won't be going on his merry way today."

"Really, sir?" she said.

The man nodded slowly as she regarded his sandy locks, his grim, determined countenance, and the purplish bruise on his nose.

The driver pulled the coach to a stop. The horseman trotted up to the side of the coach and dismounted. He stood a few yards from the carriage's door, holding one pistol and standing so that the passengers could see the sheathed saber at his side and another pistol tucked into the wide leather belt encircling his burgundy doublet. "Hand over your money and your jewels!" he commanded.

The two older gentlemen in the coach frowned as they fished their purses out of their

waistcoats.   The woman began to undo her
necklace. As the highwayman reached in to collect
the bounty, an arm stretched straight out at his eye
level, holding a pistol.

"You are under arrest in the name of the
Crown. Just put your pistols down and step back, or
I will blow your head off. And I will do it with the
greatest of pleasure."

It was Stewart, out of uniform. A trap!

Blackfriar moved carefully and deliberately
to place both his pistols onto the ground.

Then, in an instant, he quickly rose up and
flung his wrist against Stewart's forearm, slamming
it against the coach's door frame and causing the
pistol to discharge into the air. Blackfriar stepped
back to retrieve one of his own loaded pistols from
the dirt, but as he reached for it, a sharp saber blade
stabbed the dirt next to it.

Blackfriar stepped back and quickly drew
his saber to face Stewart, who had emerged from
the coach, saber drawn. Stewart slashed at him
fiercely. Blackfriar was compelled to take a few
steps backward and block his furious blows. Their
blades clashed, ringing. Stewart was not an adept
fencer—he hacked in anger rather than thrust with
skill. He swung furiously, clumsily. Blackfriar
lithely stepped aside from some blows and parried
others.

Stewart   drove   relentlessly   forward.
Blackfriar dodged and blocked and parried.
Without being able to reach his pistol on the

ground, Blackfriar's hope was to disarm the lieutenant. He ducked a swing from Stewart, then thrust back at Stewart's midsection, which Stewart narrowly evaded. Blackfriar stepped over toward the side of the coach, and, predictably, Stewart swung at him. Blackfriar ducked, and the fiercely-swung blade lodged itself in the side panel of the coach for a moment, just long enough for Blackfriar to slam Stewart across the face with the broad, curved steel hand guard of his saber. Stewart's head popped backward, and Blackfriar struck him again. Stewart began to slump downward, and Blackfriar thumped him on the back of the head with the pommel of his sword.

The lieutenant sank to the ground at the side of the coach, unconscious.

The highwayman sheathed his sword, picked up his pistols, and proceeded to retrieve the purses and jewels of the passengers.

"You're not going to kill him?" one of the men said.

"No. I'm not a murderer. I'm just hungry."

He mounted his horse and rode off.

Bess stared out the window of her small room at the full moon, its luminous glow bathing the heather in the distance.

I'll come by moonlight, he had told her.

She dried the few tears she had shed and took deep breaths, trying to calm her swirling emotions.

She had told Will not to return here, for his safety as well as hers. He had rapped on the window in the early morning the previous day to see her, and told her that he needed one more run— just one more. Then she should pack her bag.

She had written and rewritten the note she would leave for her father. It pained her to imagine his reaction. Try as she might, she could not find the words to convey her certainty that she was doing the right thing, and that the money she would leave him would be more than enough to pay off his debts and retire in comfort. She shook off the nagging feeling that she was abandoning him. She told herself that she would see her father again. That she would write. That it would all work out.

It was too late for anything else. The die was cast. She had made up her mind to go off with this highwayman. The prospect thrilled her. Her horse was saddled and her bag packed. She only awaited his arrival.

Watch for me by moonlight.

She heard hoof beats down the road. She held her breath. Was he coming?

No, wait! It was not the sound of a lone rider. It was the thunder of many horses.

Bess' heart sank at what she beheld next. A dozen redcoat soldiers rode up to the inn—in the company of Lieutenant Stewart!

Tim rushed out from the corral to greet the party. "Is he here yet?" Stewart said to him. Tim shook his head.

"You're sure it's tonight?"

"Oh, yessir," Tim said.

"And you've told no one?" The boy shook his head again.

"Good," Stewart said. "We're on time." He placed several silver coins into Tim's outstretched palm. "You've been very helpful. Now stay out of the way. There's a good lad."

Stewart and his men stormed into the inn. He raised his hands and announced to the patrons, "Ladies and gents, you might want to finish your meals and go. There will be an arrest here tonight, and it may not be pleasant."

Arthur came out from behind the bar and said, "What's all this? What's going on?"

Stewart waved his gloved hand officiously, and two soldiers seized Arthur and bound and gagged him. He thrashed about, red-faced, until a soldier smacked him down with a musket stock.

"What are you doing!?" Bess stood at the base of the staircase, screaming, eyes agape. "Leave him alone!"

"Ah, the lady herself," Stewart said. "You two"—he pointed to two privates—"take her upstairs and keep her quiet!"

The two privates seized Bess and roughly dragged her up the stairs and into one of the rooms that had a window view down to the foreyard and road below.

"Let me go!" she cried, struggling to get free.

"Sit down," said the surly private.

He stuffed a dirty cloth into her mouth . She protested, mutely, through the gagging.

He pulled up a chair and thrust her down onto it. He then produced some rope and handed a section to the other private, saying "Hold her."

"What're you doing, Harris?" said one of them.

"Jus' hold her tight." Harris bound her upper arms and torso to the chair back securely with one cord. As he bent down to use another to tie her ankles, he said, "Lieutenant Stewart ain't the only one with a grudge. Y'see, miss, that outlaw embarrassed me downstairs that night, too. Damned if I'm gonna miss my shot at him because I have to mind you. The lieutenant told me to make sure you didn't get away or cry out, but he didn't say how." He chuckled devilishly.

He inched the chair up to the window ledge so that she could clearly see out the window. He then took a loaded musket and lashed it to her body, the end of its barrel a few inches below her chin. He tested to see that it was securely in place, then ran a string snugly from its trigger to her wrist, bound behind her back. He cocked the hammer and stood back to survey his handiwork.

"Now ya see?" he gloated. "Ye've got a little breathing room, but that's it. Ye can't cry out to him because he won't hear ye. And if ye try to move, ye'll set off the musket and blow yer pretty head off. Get the picture? The only thing ye can do is sit still and watch it all." He chortled, his greasy grimace repellent to her.

She strained at her bonds, but to no avail. She could move only a little, for fear of tripping the trigger. She gave vent to a muffled cry of rage and despair, perspiration beading on her forehead and moistening her hands. Tears streamed down her smooth cheek.

"Ye'd best be still if ye wanna get through this, little lady. We wouldn't want ye all tired out for the fun afterwards." Private Harris chuckled again. "Yer sure he's comin' tonight, right? For your sake, I hope he doesn't take too long to get here."

Time crawled by. To Bess, it seemed that it must be morning, yet the bright, full moon was high in the sky.

At length, off in the distance, she heard the clattering of an approaching horseman. He was coming!

She screamed, but her screams were muffled in her throat by the gagging. She struggled, but her bonds were too tight. She could not get loose.

The galloping grew louder. *Tlot, tlot, tlot!*— were they deaf, that they did not hear?

Through the window, she could see him emerge from the darkness in the distance, a figure bathed in moonlight, furiously charging down the road—riding into a trap.

She had to warn him. But how?

Down in the yard, Lieutenant Stewart stared down the road intently, his nose still discolored, his head still sore, and his ego still bruised from the thrashings he had received from Blackfriar. Suddenly Bess heard him shout, "There he is! Look alive! Ready …aim… wait till he's close!"

A dozen redcoats hid behind barrels, fences, and sheds. A dozen muskets, cocked and readied, were raised to a dozen shoulders.

Blackfriar approached, his steed's hooves clopping.

Nervous privates sighted down their looming target, distant in the moonlight, waiting for the order.

He is riding into certain death! Bess thought.

Distraught, Bess could bear the wait no longer. She resolved to do the only thing she could do. She worked her fingers, nervously, desperately, until they found the cord tied to the trigger. She yanked her wrists, tugging at the cord.

The musket discharged, shattering her breast in the moonlight.

Soldiers down below shouted and cast about, seeking the source of the shot.

From the stable yard, Tim looked up and gasped as he saw Bess collapse upon the window sill, drenching the casement in her blood.

Blackfriar, hearing the shot, yanked at the reins of his steed. The horse reared up upon its hind legs and whinnied in protest, its front hooves clawing the night air. He turned his mount and spurred away down the road in the direction whence he had come.

In an instant, the soldiers in the yard climbed onto their horses and took off in frenzied pursuit. A moment later the ones who had been upstairs emerged from the inn and dashed out into the yard to follow on their mounts.

Stewart galloped off into the lead, charging furiously down the road after his quarry. He could see the faint moonlit outline of Blackfriar ahead, and was desperate not to lose him in the darkness beyond.

Blackfriar looked back to see the soldiers pursuing him in the distance. He scarcely had a moment to think about what had just happened. Who had warned him of the trap? Was it Bess? How? He egged his horse on faster, though the animal was wearied from the long ride to the inn.

Hooves thundered, pummeling the roadway behind him.

Stewart spurred his horse faster, harder. "Get close!" he shouted to his men, drawing his pistol. Stewart picked up speed, raking his horse's sides with his spurs, until he closed in within yards of the fleeing highwayman.

Stewart leveled his pistol, centering it on the highwayman's back, holding it as steadily as he could on his galloping mount, and fired.

The ball stung Blackfriar in the shoulder. He arched his back and let his reins slack. It was but a moment before more soldiers rode into range and fired another and another pistol and musket ball into the fugitive. Blackfriar jerked and reeled from bullet after bullet, until he tumbled headlong from his saddle onto the road.

His burgundy doublet stained with blood, and a bunch of lace at his throat, he lay like a dog shot down on the highway.

Back at the inn, Tim, the slow-witted stable boy, wept.

Afterword to "The Highwayman"

This story came to me through Phil Ochs' recording, which is a musical retelling of the Alfred Noyes poem.

I had been interested in writing in high school, but when I got into college and for thirty-five years after that, I never did any creative writing. I had no ideas. Then when I started to get into Phil Ochs, I was struck by the imagery and power of this story and thought that maybe I could flesh it out as a short story. It would be an interesting exercise and maybe get the creative juices flowing.

Well, that didn't quite happen. I eventually got into writing other stories instead, and years passed. But this was always on the back burner and still appealed to me. So in February, 2011, when nothing else was coming and I hadn't written for a while, I sat down to try to hammer out at least the beginning. I had the backstory in mind of why the highwayman turned to robbery. I made a little progress when I got sidetracked into "Jerry." I worked on both of them simultaneously for a while, and when I finished that one, I returned to this one and the juices at long last started flowing and it progressed the way the other stories progressed.

I call this my "bodice-ripper," my version of the tale of a rogue outlaw and a tavern wench. I like the English moor / old country inn setting. I like being able to use words like "tankard" and "bodice" and "musket." I got the name Blackfriar from a sign in London. I also incorporated phrases from the original poem and song when I could, including references to the wine-red tunic, the moon, shattering her breast in the moonlight, etc. It just struck me as very evocative.

And still on a winter's night, they say, when the wind is in the trees,
When the moon is a ghostly galleon tossed upon cloudy seas,
When the road is a gypsy's ribbon looping the purple moor,
The highwayman comes riding...
Riding...riding
The highwayman comes riding, up to the old inn-door.